THE TERRIBLE FIVES

THE TERRIBLE Fives

a novel by

ISHMAEL REED

Includes the essay

MY FLIGHT TO CANADA

Baraka Books

Montréal

All rights reserved. No part of this publication may be used in conjunction with large language modelling or other artificial intelligence, including for training or text analysis, or be reproduced or transmitted in any form or by any means without permission in writing from the publisher.

© Ishmael Reed

Editor: Robin Philpot
Cover: Leila Marshy
Book design: Folio infographie

ISBN 978-177186-397-1 pbk
ISBN 978-1-77186-455-8 epub
ISBN 978-1-77186-456-5 pdf

Legal Deposit, 4th quarter 2026
Bibliothèque et Archives nationales du Québec
Library and Archives Canada

Published Baraka Books

TRADE DISTRIBUTION & RETURNS
Canada – UTPdistribution.com
United States & World – Independent Publishers Group: IPGbook.com

This, we have been reminded, was the dream Kennedy nourished, and much of it died with him, when the sharp cracks of rifle fire broke out as his motorcade rolled through the sunstruck streets of Dallas. With this horrific, irrational deed, a curse was laid upon the land, and the people fell from grace.

By Sam Tanenhaus, Nov. 21, 2013, The New York Times

My Flight to Canada

Author stands before Willem de Kooning's painting of JFK.
(Photo by Tennessee Reed.)

My Flight to Canada

After I resigned from running a newspaper in Newark, I decided to begin my first novel. Under pressure from Black musicians and painters, who are still the avant-garde, I felt I'd have to do something different. In my late teens, I'd been influenced by Nathaniel West's *A Cool Million* and *The Dream Life of Balso Snell,* which applied the techniques of collage to writing. The New York painters with whom I was close were also collagists. I saw my approach to the novel as influenced more by painters and musicians than by novelists. I also decided to work with popular genres rather than the classics. Pop, gothic film, the western, the whodunit, the detective novel, and the slave narrative for which I coined the term "The Neo Slave Narrative" in a 1984 interview with the late critic Reginald Martin, and sometimes hybrids—the Washington novel, fused with a Christmas novel.

Because Langston Hughes and editor Anne Freedgood admired my work, my first novel, *The Free-Lance Pallbearers,* was published in 1967.

I was 29 and living in New York. Some reacted hostilely because I was seen as someone who leaped to the head of the line. To avoid the flak, I removed myself from the New York literary scene—I was 29—by moving to California, instead of waiting to be adopted as a token Divo by those who set trends in American writing. Such a process is still happening, according to Howard

Rambsy II and Kenton Rambsy's "How the 'New York Times' Covers Black Writers," in *Public Books magazine*, 10 Dec. 2022.

Pallbearers, like my other novels, received mixed reviews, ranging from serious consideration by Michel Fabre, a critic and Sorbonne professor (*Ishmael Reed's The Freelance Pallbearers, or, The Dialectics of Shit*), to *Kirkus Reviews*, whose reviewer wrote that the book should be flushed down the toilet and the author with it.

Doubleday published my first three novels, *The Free-Lance Pallbearers*, *Yellow Back Radio Broke-Down*, and *Mumbo Jumbo*. *Mumbo Jumbo* received critical acclaim, which included a front-page review in *The New York Times Book Review*.

My attorney, Ellis Freedman, and I met with Doubleday brass about a $40,000 advance for my next novel. Instead, Ken McCormick, my editor at Doubleday after Anne Freedgood left for Random House, said they'd prefer I write a non-fiction book about Jimi Hendrix and brought in a Black man named Larry Jordan to tell me how much of a commercial failure *Mumbo Jumbo* was. McCormick was Truman and Eisenhower's editor. My style puzzled him. He was comfortable with Faulkner's modernism.

I told them to hire poet David Henderson to write the book. David Henderson was glad to get the assignment and even gave me a hundred-dollar finder's fee. His biography of Hendrix, *Scuse Me While I Kiss The Sky: Jimi Hendrix: Voodoo Child*, has sold over 500,000 copies.

Since I had decided to continue writing novels, Anne Freedgood, my Doubleday editor, invited me to continue my career at Random House, where she'd landed a job. I became friendly with Toni Morrison, who had taken Charles Harris's place. Harris became editor at Howard University Press. He founded Amistad Press, which is still functioning. He and John A. Williams published two issues of the magazine *Amistad*. It was Harris who brought *The Greatest*, Muhammad Ali's autobiography, written by Richard Durham, to Random House.

It was apparent that Random House would be lukewarm to the kind of novels I was able to publish at Doubleday. Appearing on a panel covered by *The New York Times* on February 22, 1981, under the heading "Hard Times for Black Writers," Toni said the kind of "experimental" novel that I wrote didn't sell.

As Toni Morrison pointed out, "the decrease in the number of published novels by Black authors can partly be explained by the publishing industry's economic problems. In the past," she said, "publishers could underwrite experimental fiction and special market fiction with profits made from more successful books. But that happens less frequently now. The problem is that the small bookseller cannot afford to take marginal novels."

Perhaps this is why Toni rejected Charles Wright's *The Wig* with one sentence and William Demby's *Love Story Black*, both of which are now considered classics.

Walter Bowart, with whom I co-founded the underground newspaper *The East Village Other*, married Peggy Mellon Hitchcock, the heiress. He invited Carla Blank and me for dinner. Among the guests was John Sargent, the then-president of Doubleday. Actor Rex Harrison's ex-wife served dinner. We shared a cab with

Sargent. He told me that Doubleday received tax deductions for the kind of books I wrote. Apparently, Nelson Doubleday felt the same way. He was rude to Carla and me at a San Francisco event the company hosted.

Toni Morrison was so upset with my novel, *The Last Days of Louisiana Red,* that she bawled me out in front of the Random House staff. Not only was the novel "experimental," but at that point in her career she insisted that all Black women characters be positive, a rule that she disobeyed in *Tar Baby*, a brilliant novel, maybe her best, and a rule that Zora Neale Hurston also ignored.

Nevertheless, *The Last Days of Louisiana Red* was a Book of the Month selection and received my first major award, the Rosenthal Award from the National Institute of Arts and Letters. And though Anne Freedgood remained my advocate at Random House, she didn't have the power to convince the sales department, which even put pressure on Toni Morrison. When readers found inconsistencies in *Paradise*, one of her novels, she explained that she had been rushed by salespersons to get it out by Christmas.

Despite the honors *The Last Days of Louisiana Red* received, there was little promotion. The publicity director at Random House told *Esquire* that she saw her job as promoting Black women writers. This is still the case. Elizabeth Nunez, an underrated writer, told *Poets and Writers* before her death that publishers wanted "girlfriend books" from Black writers.

My final book with Random House was *Flight to Canada*, which was also dismissed as an "experimental" novel and unsaleable. The 50th anniversary edition of

Mumbo Jumbo was published by Scribner in 2022, and the 50th anniversary of *Flight to Canada* was published by Scribner in August 2026. My books, considered commercial failures at the time of publication, tend to hang around.

My next stop was St. Martin's Press. It's happened more than once in my career that the beginning of a novel or theater project conjures a series of coincidences that coincide with the novel or play's theme. While writing the book for the "Gospera," eventually titled *Gethsemane Park*, a work that was performed by Black singers who were trained in the European tradition, and gospel singers trained in the Black tradition, I was invited to Israel, where I found myself in the Garden of Gethsemane. The Gospera was originally commissioned by the San Francisco Opera Company, but the composer, famous for his popular music, wasn't able to write the score. The libretto rights reverted to me, and I hired composer Carman Moore to write the music, which he created within three months. Carman was elected to the American Academy of Arts and Letters in 2023.

My interpretation of the arrest of Jesus in the Garden of Gethsemane became so controversial that I earned one-third of my investment by defending the book at the Union Theological Seminary and the Institute for Signifying Scriptures. I was also invited to the Union Theological Institute to discuss my book. After viewing the Gospera, the late Reverend Calvin Butts said he liked the music but had problems with the book, "but that's Ishmael." However, he said he'd preach a sermon about the book questioning why Lazarus would want to return to earth after experiencing paradise. A video of the Gospera was shown at a white fundamentalist church in Hampton, Virginia, on Good Friday. The following Monday, the minister who requested it be shown there was fired. Something similar happened when I began writing *The Terrible Twos* after overhearing a guest at a New York Party refer to a Black assistant as St. Nicholas. I began researching the legend and began writing a novel about the relationship. Coincidentally, I received an invitation from Jos Knipscheer, my Dutch publisher, to attend a festival in Amsterdam, inspired by the Before Columbus Foundation, a coalition of writers that I founded in 1976, the year of *Flight to Canada*'s publication.

While there, I witnessed the arrival of Nicholas and Black Peter in the harbor, accompanied by Senoritas, because the legend says Nicholas, Black Peter, and their entourage arrived from Spain. Peter, who wears a Moor's costume, probably first arrived with the occupation of the Netherlands by Spain.

The actor playing Nicholas mounted a white horse, and his aide, a white man in blackface, climbed into a sports car and began hurling gifts at the children who were yelling his name and ignoring Nicholas. I took photos of the ceremony. I decided to combine the Dickensian Christmas novel with books and films about Washington intrigue, like the classic and prophetic *Seven Days in May*, whose screenplay was written by Rod Serling.

The Terrible Twos was published in 1982 to a rave review in *The New York Times* by the late John Leonard,

Black Peter.

but in an indication of what was to come, feminist Elizabeth Pochoda sponsored a hit on the book by Stanley Crouch, who'd been assigned by the Neo Con literary establishment to maintain the Manhattan literary status quo and to knock down any challenge to its monopoly by Black writers. His inauguration came in print form, *The Partisan Review*, 1996, Vol. 63. His bid for the assignment was accepted by his fellow forum members, which included the late historian Arthur M. Schlesinger, who was among those who doted over Stanley's expression "tragic optimism," which no one, including Stanley, defined during the forum. Like his fellow official historians, great white man groupies, Schlesinger wrote his book, *The Age of Jackson*, without any mention of "The Trail Of Tears," which saw the mass evacuation of the Cherokee and their Black slaves from their traditional homeland. In the 1950s and 60s *The Partisan Review* was supported by the C.I.A.

Feminist Elizabeth Podocha hired Stanley Crouch to comment on my misogyny in what was supposed to be a review of *The Terrible Twos*. In it, he made sarcastic remarks about the Before Columbus Foundation, dismissing it as "Ishmael Reed's literary army." Since then, members of the army have become part of the literary canon.

It was this review that convinced me that white feminists and their surrogates would scapegoat Black male writers for misogyny while remaining silent about misogyny taking place among their ethnic groups or practiced by those who could advance their careers or the men who could decide whether they received tenure.

Despite other positive reviews in *The Times*, *The Terrible Twos* found no enthusiasm from St. Martin's. I had planned to proceed with *The Terrible Threes*, but sensed momentum, among academics and feminists who were authors and public intellectuals, to single out Black men to take the rap for American misogyny.

Feminist bell hooks agreed with me. She wrote,

> Fundamentally, Reed is critically on the mark when he calls attention to a differentiation in reactions to black and white male sexism within the feminist movement. Contemporary feminists do tend to act as though black male sexism is more heinous than white male sexism of much of the feminist movement; it is not surprising that the early radical focus on rape tended to project the racist stereotype that the male most to be feared was black.

She continued,

> Listening to mature feminists make similar comments about Reed and other black male writers, I call to their willingness to pass judgment on black male writers when it is rare to hear such condemnation of white male writers. Within literary studies, racism often shapes this response. White women who study racism often shape this response. White women who cannot imagine excluding Chaucer, Shakespeare, or Joyce from their reading list, even though their works reflect sexism and racism, easily use this criterion to defend their ignorance of writing by black men. Currently, in the academic world, the trend among women interested in critical theory, or post-colonial discourse, is to overlook as much as possible the sexism and racism of white male thinkers—Derrida, Foucault, Jameson, and Said, for example.

Reckless Eyeballing was a satire about a Manhattan feminist's claim that Emmett Till, for whistling at Carolyn Bryant Donham (she lied), made him just as guilty as the men who murdered him. Susan Brownmiller claimed that when construction workers ogled her as Till was supposed to have ogled Donham, she was seized with a "murderous rage."

The Village Voice was Black male-bashing central at one time. A Black feminist who wrote for the publication told me that feminist Karen Durbin encouraged Black women who wrote for the newspaper to attack Black men. Ms. Durbin seemed comfortable with her position at the *Voice* despite the demonstrations against the *Voice* for carrying ads for *Backpage.com*, "adult ads that were accused of facilitating sex trafficking."

Michele Wallace had predicted my vanishing from the mainstream in 1986 when she told the kind of people who read *The Village Voice*,

> Reed was next up for inclusion in the canon in the 70s, but his career appears to be in decline—precipitated, in no small part, by his perversely misogynistic views. Despite his popularity among black male critics, his novels receive less and less media attention, and all of his books except *Reckless Eyeballing* are now out of print, which doesn't bode well for canon inclusion.

She was right. My literary efforts were like the Little Richard song where the Canon says to me, "Keep a knockin' but you can't come in." But was *The Village Voice* the right place to air my misogyny?

IRANGATE: WHERE IS THE *TIMES*? (PRESS CLIPS, P. 10)

the village VOICE

THE WEEKLY NEWSPAPER OF NEW YORK

THE WHOLE BRUCE CATALOGUE
(Marshall Berman, P. 87)

VLS
VOICE LITERARY SUPPLEMENT

THE RISE OF A NEW BLACK CULTURE
BY GREG TATE

ISHMAEL REED'S FEMALE TROUBLES
BY MICHELE WALLACE

THE THREE FACES OF ANNE RICE
BY DOROTHY ALLISON

Sneak Preview: Enrique Fernández on García Márquez's New Novel

COUP D'ETAT
How Oliver North Seized the White House (Ridgeway, P. 22)
An Interview With Nicaragua's Veep (Paul Berman, P. 28)
The End of the Reagan Era (Mark Green, P. 26)

WE TOLD YOU SO
The Disgrace of Stanley Friedman (Barrett, P. 14) (Newfield, P. 16)

A TRADER TO HIS CLASS
Scott Malcomson on Ivan Boesky, Capitalist Fool (P. 31)

FURY (MARCUS ON ROBERT JOHNSON, P. 63)

This was a newspaper that was boycotted for carrying back-page ads where pedophiles could find information about sex with children. The newspaper was picketed for running these ads. *The Village Voice* was published by white men. One of whom stabbed his wife. The brown one.

The Voice even accused James Baldwin of putting "woman-hating lines" in the speeches of characters in his novel *If Beale Street Could Talk.*

Men also owned *The New Republic*, where I have been hit three times by Barbara Smith, Victoria Bond, and Jennifer Wilson. I'm sure that their criticism was well-intentioned, but were they aware that *The New Republic* endorsed *The Bell Curve*, a quack effort about Black intellectual inferiority? Andrew Sullivan's endorsement of the book led to the resignation of some who worked there. *The Bell Curve* was financed by the Pioneer Fund, which has been accused of Nazi ties. Moreover, Marty Peretz, *The New Republic's* owner, said in 1994 that "So many people in the Black population are afflicted by deficiencies. And I mean, cultural deficiencies, which Jews, for example, don't have."

Jeet Heer, a national affairs correspondent for *The Nation* and former staff writer for *The New Republic*, wrote about *The New Republic*'s history in his "*The New Republic*'s Legacy on Race: From DuBois to the Bell Curve." Unlike the old days, when *The New Republic* referred to Blacks as "niggers," a more sinister kind of racism was introduced by Marty Peretz. Heer writes:

> Marty Peretz's magazine was attributing the problems of black America to Jesse Jackson, Marion Barry, and

anonymous welfare mothers, while largely ignoring deindustrialization and mass incarceration. Affirmative action became a regular target; legacy admission of whites to colleges and universities was rarely discussed. Of course, the competing positions on affirmative action deserved an airing. But to attack affirmative action in a magazine with a staff that was almost entirely white and male was to defend not a principle but a troubling status quo. One of the most serious offenses against Blacks like Margaret Seltzer's *Love and Consequences* (2008) praised by Michiko Kakutani, was a fake.

In 1998, Stephen Glass penned a 1996 piece about the Washington, D.C. taxi cab industry that seemed to cater to Peretz's appetite for melodramas illustrating black cultural pathology. The article drew an invidious contrast between hard-working, uncomplaining immigrants who believed in the American dream versus entitled black Americans who spurned honest work (and chased after white women). The piece included imaginary details such as, "Four months ago, a 17-year-old held a gun to Eswan's head while his girlfriend performed oral sex on the gunman." Glass also claimed to be in a cab when a young African American man mugged the driver, and celebrated the exploits of a fictional Kae Bang, the 'Korean cab-driver-turned-vigilante' who used martial arts to beat up black teenagers who tried to rob his cab. It's fair to say that Glass's fabrications in this piece and others did more damage to *The New Republic* than any event in its history. And it's hard to accept a piece like the above would have been published in a magazine which wasn't already inclined toward a pernicious view of African Americans.

I found it futile to contest the misstatements about my views made by Barbara Smith and Victoria Bond because their editors protected them from scrutiny. Bond said that I called *The Color Purple* a Nazi conspiracy. I wrote a correction to her editor, Chloe Schama, who said they didn't print letters, but I could respond with an article. I sent an article from Paris. Schama, now at *Vogue*, said she didn't have time to edit it. So the lie stood. Was Schama on the staff of *The New Republic* when Leon Wieseltier, the editor, was fired for sexual harassment? When he had a serious cocaine problem?

Recently, my critics, Amanda Gorman and Salamishah Tillet, have problems with me, yet they're OK with *Hamilton* about a man who sold at least one Black woman and her child for over $200. Four women historians had criticized *Hamilton* for omitting Alexander Hamilton's career as a slaveowner. I merely staged their research. Ms. Tillet, a PhD recipient, Pulitzer Prize winner, columnist for *The New York Times*, and member of the Alice Walker womanist cult, was criticized by Jennifer Wilson in *The New Republic* for being soft on Walker's anti-Semitism. Wilson also criticized my calling Walker Gloria Steinem's "pawn" in an Australian newspaper. I asked her to send me the name and date of the Australian newspaper. She still hasn't answered.

Maybe she got me mixed up with Toni Morrison, who said in the *University of Massachusetts Review* that nobody would have heard of *The Color Purple* without Gloria Steinem's promotion. While defending Ms. Steinem, though, Ms. Wilson mentioned serial rapist Harvey Weinstein but didn't comment on the irony of

Weinstein investing in the musical version of *The Color Purple*, in which Black men, according to *Times* film critic Alissa Wilkinson, published Dec. 19, 2023, and updated Jan. 2, 2024, are depicted as "soulless monsters."

Maybe not satisfied with the job her womanist surrogates were doing in my career, Alice Walker, who supports David Icke, a holocaust denier, attacked my mother in her book *Gathering Blossoms Under Fire*.

I wrote a letter that was sent to the book's publisher by my New York attorney, Jesse Bueno. We're still waiting for an apology from Simon and Schuster.

> Dear Simon and Schuster,
> Alice Walker's new book *Gathering Blossoms Under Fire* includes the following scene:
>
> > "I think Toni does have a brilliant, dark power, that she is more comfortable studying evil than I. I can study confusion, which most times only looks like evil, & I'd have a hard time even mentally choking a dog. She was also very kind in her remarks about Ishmael Reed, saying she could never take him seriously. She seems to have known him for a long time and recently had dinner with him. She explained that when Ishmael was a little boy, around 5, his mother took him to meet his father, 'a successful businessman' who threw them out of his office. This was Ishmael's first meeting with his father. I said this story explains I's hatred of black women writers: we keep taking him to meet his father."
>
> My mother, Thelma V. Reed, wrote her own book, *Black Girl From Tannery Flats*. Since Ms. Walker has powerful contacts in both publishing and academia, her charge has been very costly to me. Is there any way we can rectify

this situation? By the way, I'm listed on your website as a Simon and Schuster author.

Sincerely,

Ishmael Reed
Distinguished Professor, California College of the Arts

This scene she describes never happened, and the line that I hate Black women writers can be refuted by the scores of Black women writers I've published. My last four honors were bestowed upon me by organizations led by Black women, the most recent being the Hurston/Wright Award. Two foundations I founded have honored Black women writers. My daughter, Tennessee, is the managing editor of our zine, *Konch*, which began as a print publication in 1990. We asked writers from China, Japan, South Africa, Nigeria, England, Canada, and the United States their personal responses to Covid. The response was so overwhelming that we published the two issues in book form, including a piece by Margaret Busby, one of several Black women contributors. Margaret Busby is my English publisher. My agent, Faith Childs is a Black woman,

My late mother single-handedly organized two strikes that benefitted Black women. She wrote as well as Alice Walker (*Black Girl from Tannery Flats*). Also, my mother would have never accepted a dime from Harvey Weinstein.

Gloria Steinem used her review of Walker's *The Color Purple*, which was full of vicious attacks on Black male writers, to drive Black male writers out of the market, the living and the dead ones. They even went after Richard Wright, but his greatness escaped their blows.

My Oakland lawyer agreed with my New York attorney that her remarks were libelous, but how am I, with limited funds, supposed to fight a publishing giant like Simon & Schuster? Would Simon & Schuster have treated a white male author this way? Put out a lie about his deceased mother without fact checking with the author? Is this another example of a double standard?

Former Senator Claire McCaskill said that the men involved in the Epstein scandal were being protected because they are white and rich, implying that if they were Black or Brown, their names would have been exposed. Indeed, they'd probably have received jail time. Crowds of feminists showed up for the Congressional hearings for Supreme Court Justice Clarence Thomas, the trial of Bill Cosby, and P. Diddy and others, but have not shown up in Washington now that some of the most powerful men in the West are involved in pedophilia.

According to Harriet Fraad, writing in *Tikkun*, a movement that began as working-class and integrated was co-opted by Gloria Steinem. The same can be said of the Gay movement. Whenever the press prints stories about the Stonewall revolt, they include pictures of white faces when those who started the revolt were Black and Puerto Rican. The Gay movement did a white-over. When my critic Barbara Smith joined the Gay march in Washington, the white Gay leadership told her to get lost because they were interested in mainstreaming not Civil Rights.

So what did real writers think about *Reckless Eyeballing*? Toni Morrison and Adrienne Kennedy, whose play *The Ohio State Murders* reached Broadway in 2022, were in attendance at the book's launch party,

Tony Morrison and Adrienne Kennedy. (Photo by Ishmael Reed.)

and Pulitzer Prize winner Gwendolyn Brooks gave me the George Kent Award for the book. Jamaica Kincaid told an Italian newspaper that I was her favorite writer.

But *Reckless Eyeballing* raised the ire of third-and fourth-tier feminist and womanist writers who didn't read it but formed their views based on negative reviews in *The Village Voice* and *The New York Times.* I wasn't surprised that some feminists who'd threatened to boycott my appearance at the University of Louisiana at Baton Rouge hadn't read the books they were boycotting. This was typical of feminist critics of *Reckless Eyeballing.*

Patrick McGee, author of *Ishmael Reed and the Ends of Race,* wrote:

> Having just finished reading all of his novels, I was surprised to learn that Reed himself, at the invitation of some creative writing faculty, was coming to Louisiana State University early in the semester to give a talk. I also

> learned that some of my colleagues were opposed to this invitation (which had been arranged without the participation of the whole faculty) and had decided to organize a boycott of the talk. I found that only a few of them had read any of Reed's work and were basing their response to him almost exclusively on his reputation for misogyny. When I contacted a well-known feminist at another university to get her opinion, I was surprised to hear her say that she would never attend a talk by Reed, though she confessed that she had never read any of his work. In this way, it became clear to me that reading Ishmael Reed could be a political act in more than a theoretical sense.

Judged as anti-feminist, one of the few characters in the book with any kind of integrity is the feminist character Tremonisha Smarts, whose portrait critics heard through the rumor mill was against Black women, a rumor which reached Martinque where I received a chilly reception on my second visit as a guest lecturer at the University des Antilles-Guyana. As McGee noted,

> Ian Ball, by the end of *Reckless Eyeballing*, shows himself to have far less integrity than Tremonisha Smarts. She leaves New York rather than have white critics and producers take over her work, but Ian willingly sells his artistic independence to achieve success. If anyone in *Reckless Eyeballing* betrays his "race" and collaborates with the enemy, it is the man who humiliates black women by night and peddles his talent to white women by day. In fact, Reed paints a more unflattering portrait of the male African-American artist than can be found in any novel by a black feminist.

The Terrible Threes was published in 1989. Rebbeca Pepper Sinkler, a feminist who was then editor of *The*

Times Book Review, hired Gerald Early, a friend of Stanley Crouch, to review the book. He had been critical of my previous works. He criticized my interest in boxing in a book about boxing, yet printed my essay about the second Spinks-Ali fight without paying me. He told the *St. Louis Post-Dispatch* that he and Stanley Crouch decided that I had been replaced by novelist Charles Johnson.

So it was predictable that he would snuff *The Terrible Threes*. He dismissed *The Terrible Threes* with an attention-grabbing line. He wrote, "Mr. Reed, in his latest novel, has finally reached the impasse of actually writing a novel that truly does not make sense." Responsible and ethical reviewers who actually read the novel and incorporated the storyline and characters into their reviews had no trouble making sense of it.

I shouldn't have been surprised that this kind of flip remark would pass as a review. In a bizarre incident, the feminist Rebecca Pepper Sinkler, who assigned the novel to the reviewer crashed a luncheon I had arranged with Brent Staples, former book reviewer for *The Times*, and spent the whole time lauding the literary achievements of Toni Morrison. Though Staples had written a hostile review of *Reckless Eyeballing*—he said my books were punched out, rather than written—he and I have had a friendly relationship. Elizabeth Pochoda, who assigned Stanley Crouch to do a flip dismissal of my novel in *The Nation*, cited Philip Roth as her mentor. Roth was responsible for her obtaining a job at *The Nation* and when he asked her for sex, she didn't go full Me Too on him but was flattered. Rebecca Pepper Sinkler, who assigned Gerald Early to obliterate *The Terrible Threes,* also cited Philip Roth as her "friend and mentor" in *The New York Times* on June 28, 2026. When asked by *Esquire* how he expected feminists to respond to a novel written by him, he said, "fuck the feminists." Toni Morrison told me that "The Family" an aggregate of New York cultural interests that have imposed Divas and Divos on Black literature for over 100 years, resented her receiving the Nobel Prize for literature. They wanted Roth to win.

The contradictions of bourgeois feminism don't end there. Feminist lawyer Susan Estrich wrote a pioneering work criticizing the way police handle rape cases, yet she's representing Leon Black, who's been accused by Epstein survivors of rape, and before that, she represented a sexual predator, the late Roger Ailes. Is this like feminist Lisa Bloom offering to represent Harvey Weinstein and The Black Womanists, a clique led by an anti-Semite accepting money from him? When will working-class feminists rescue their movement?

For Michiko Kakutani and Rebecca Pepper Sinkler, I was taking up space they'd reserved for Morrison, with whom I maintained a friendship until my last conversation with her as she lay dying. Our last words: I said, "Toni, Jesus is not finished with you," and she replied, "And I'm not finished with him." I was living in her Manhattan apartment at the time. Otherwise, we would have had to spend thousands of dollars in a hotel while rehearsing for my play, *The Haunting of Lin-Manuel Miranda.*

On the day that the Kakutani review appeared I got a call from a friend of the family, the wife of the great

Cast and crew of *The Haunting of Lin-Manuel Miranda*.
(Photo by Tennessee Reed.)

filmmaker Allen Willis, who PBS station KQED assigned to do a documentary about my work entitled *There with Ishmael Reed*. She said that *The Times* had called me "anti-Semitic." She was Jewish and was dying of cancer, and we never spoke to each other again.

It was Kakutani who called my novel, *Reckless Eyeballing*, anti-Semitic.

> As for the New York arts world, *Reckless Eyeballing* suggests that it's a closed shop, dominated by women and Jews, in which the only artists who get ahead are those willing to pander to them and adopt fashionable views. To say the least, it's a paranoid position with disturbing implications, and it does a disservice to Mr. Reed's own notable career. (*The Times*, April 5, 1986)

Here's an example of some of the anti-Semitism in the novel. A character says:

> "Not a scapegoat. A scapegoat is one who is sacrificed to achieve a larger end. In Germany, the annihilation of the Jews was the end."

"What about this thing about the Jews killing Christ?"

"The Germans did it. The Romans brought in these German toughs to deal with the Jews, just like they used to import southern cops to deal with niggers."

"You mean the Germans did it all along? Then they blame it on the Jews?"

"Yeah. The Jews were the only ones keeping you guys going. But instead of expressing gratitude, the fellas keep coming down hard on the Jews, and commenting on the Middle East when most of you don't even know where it is on the map. Instead of fighting the Jews, you ought to be like them. They've survived all of their enemies, the Assyrians, the Babylonians, the Persians, the Pharaonic and Ptolemaic Egyptians, and Rome. All dead. In fifty years, they will have outlived the Germans, a vanishing race hung up on Föhn. Germany's population growth is zero. They don't have the will to continue. It's as though they've been obeahed or dybukked. Günter Grass has written a book about it: Headbirths, or The Germans Are Dying Out."

He kept on yammering about how the blacks ought to be like Jews. The waiter took the plates away. Ball was glad. He was really getting sick. How could Shoboater eat that shit, he thought. "These blacks ought to save their money instead of loafing around and break-dancing."

"Man, if the Jews hadn't gone in there and tried to civilize these people with their bloodthirsty Viking gods, these people would still be on the rampage. And every time there's a period of reaction against compassion and mercy, these gods start to rumble again. They even named this new laser weapon Excalibur; they can't get swords out of their minds. If Judaism hadn't required those people to renounce their bloodthirsty war gods, the world would have been finished long ago." The waiter brought Shoboater a tiny cup full of espresso. Ball was on his third Pabst.

"The V-1 rocket designed at Peenemünde was the ancestor of the modern missile. It would have enabled Hitler to strike England and the U.S. with A-bombs. He rejected the A-bomb. Called the theory behind it 'Jewish physics.' His wrongheaded bigotry finally did him in."

Those characters who spoke anti-Semitic lines were buffoons!!

Michiko Kakutani showed her prejudice towards Blacks when she endorsed Margaret Seltzer's racist memoir *Love and Consequences* (2008), about her life as a half-white, half-Native American girl growing up in South-Central Los Angeles as a foster child among gang members, running drugs for the Bloods gang. This book included the kind of stereotypes about Blacks that have been circulating for hundreds of years.

Writing in *The New York Times*, Michiko Kakutani praised Seltzer's "humane and deeply affecting memoir." This has caused an indelible stain on Kakutani's career. Writing about the fraud, *The Times*' critic Motoko Rich wrote on March 4, 2008:

The problem is that none of it is true. Margaret Jones is a pseudonym for Margaret Seltzer, who is white and grew up in the well-to-do Sherman Oaks section of Los Angeles, in the San Fernando Valley, with her biological family. She graduated from the Campbell Hall School, a private Episcopal day school in the North Hollywood neighborhood. She has never lived with a foster family, nor did she run drugs for any gangs. Nor did she graduate from the University of Oregon, as she had claimed.

So, Michiko Kakutani did a hatchet job on my novel, *Reckless Eyeballing*, but fell for a racist fake gang memoir. In this review, Kakutani exposed her racist feelings about Black culture.

The problem with the *Times* review of *The Terrible Threes*, a hit job assigned by Rebecca Sinkler, is that it killed the book, for which MacMillan had spent money in advertising and promotion. A disappointment for MacMillan editors who believed in the book. MacMillan also published my *New and Collected Poetry*, which *The Times* cited as one of the four best books of poetry in 2006. Despite feminist reviewers using surrogates to eliminate reader enthusiasm for the *Twos* and *Threes*, both books are still in print.

If Kakutani's review of *Reckless Eyeballing* was not enough, I appeared on NBC's *The Today Show* the day after the review was published. St. Martin's had flown me in to talk about my book. Instead, I was ambushed with a debate about the film *The Color Purple*, which was up for an Oscar that day. Black feminists on NBC's production team surprised me with a debating partner, the journalist Clarence Page. They asked me what I thought of the film, and I said it was the kind of film they made about Jews in Nazi Germany. I was judging by the trailers, which showed Danny Glover, the actor playing Mister, as a sexual predator. I made the parallel because I had attended a lecture sponsored by the San Francisco's JFCS Holocaust Center. The lecturer said that the Nazi media depicted

Jewish men as predators corrupting Christian women, which is the subtext of the Epstein scandal.

My book wasn't mentioned, which is why St. Martin's flew me to New York to appear on the show. When I asked one of the Black feminists to explain why my book wasn't discussed, she said that they hadn't guaranteed that it would be covered.

A *New York Times*' book reviewer quoted my comment that the feminist movement was the biggest threat to Black male survival since the Klan, because I knew that a white led feminist movement would single out Black men to take the rap for misogyny, something that Amiri Baraka pointed out. He agreed with Harriet Fraad that the Steinem faction wasn't interested in changing society; they wanted in. Baraka also mentioned their racism, something about which Black women have complained for over a hundred years. Feminists from other ethnic groups who criticize Black sexism tend to be mum about such misogyny in the ethnic groups to which they belong. I asked Beth Singer, niece of the late Issac Bashevis Singer why. She said these women are told not to reveal the secrets of the group. Also those who label me as a misogynist quote two or three women and ignore the support I receive from Native American, Hispanic, Asian American, and Black women, many of whom I've published. Recently, in my magazine *Konch*, I published two Chinese women from the mainland, their first appearance in print. And though white men and men from other ethnic groups, foxes guarding the chicken coop, become honorary Black feminists, joining the two or three of my Black feminist opponents, they have been revealed as hypocrites.

One famous Dominican American writer, Junot Diaz, apologized to me for confusing Toni Morrison with Alice Walker when writing about feuds I was supposed to have had with Black women writers in *The Boston Review.*

On Friday, June 29, 2012, Deborah Chasman of *The Boston Review* wrote:

> Hi
> I got this from Junot. Do you want to post it on your web site? He wants us to make a correction on ours.
> Deb
>
> From: Junot Diaz
> Date: June 29, 2012 1:04:56 PM EDT
> To: Deborah Chasman
> Subject: Ishmael Reed
>
> Send him the following on his website
> professor reed
>
> please forgive the error which crept into an interview which was transcribed in the middle of a conference from a poor voice recording. the sentence was supposed to be read "the very public fulminations of Stanley Crouch versus Toni Morrison, Ishmael Reed versus Alice Walker, Frank Chin versus Maxine Hong Kingston."
> And you are correct that it wasn't so simple as just men of color versus women of color, but sometimes in an interview, we don't always do the subject the nuance it deserves. and this error which put you at odds with a friend is regrettable. i meant to do no disrespect to my two great idols—please forgive. the point was simply that as an undergrad in af-am studies classes at the time these gender spats were very real and were being discussed and

> it was in these contestations, in these debates, that i began to discern gender insights that would form the the core of my art. i am so very sorry that an error on my part caused you any kind of distress. I've asked the review to correct it immediately. and i will respond publicly as well. please please forgive, professor reed.
> god, what an error, mud on my face. shit. Junot

This honorary Black feminist, Junot Diaz, got busted in 2018 for sexual aggression. He apologized attributing such aggression to a traumatic incident that occurred during in his childhood, and was forgiven and welcomed back into the Establishment maybe because his accusers were Black and Latina, who in the eyes of the white male establishment are sluts anyway, a stereotype critiqued in Yuri Kageyama's poetic masterpiece, "Little Yellow Slut" which could be "Brown Slut," and "Black Slut." Spain's *El Pais* was the only newspaper printed my Oped about how Trump won the 2024 election by smearing Kamala Harris when he called her a whore. The Black pundits knew this to be the case but were ordered by TV executives to attribute her loss to economic discontent. These pundits didn't want to get the Joy Reid, Don Lemon treatment.

The Allegations

In brief, Zinzi Clemmons, an acclaimed writer who teaches writing part-time at Occidental College, in person at an Australian writers festival and on Twitter accused Díaz of forcibly kissing her after she invited him to come speak at Columbia University when she was a graduate student there. A National Book Award finalist, Carmen Maria Machado, also tweeted that Díaz belittled her and implied that she was a "prude" for 20 minutes after she asked him about the fraught relationships with women depicted in his work, during a talk at the University of Iowa Writers' Workshop, from which she'd just graduated. Author Monica Byrne said on social media that Díaz shouted "rape" in her face during a conversation at a dinner party to prove a point, and continued to cut her off and talk over her throughout the evening.

Writer Alisa Valdes rehashed an account of Díaz she'd blogged about a decade earlier. She said that when she was a reporter in her twenties, she interviewed Díaz, who allegedly insisted on finishing the interview at her apartment. Valdes said he feigned interest in her burgeoning literary career, saying he could help her get her manuscript to the "right people" before suggesting that they have sex. They began a relationship that Valdes thought was based on mutual admiration, she said, but the romance soon faded: Díaz allegedly told her he had a girlfriend before asking her to clean up his kitchen, strewn with hundreds of iced tea bottles. You can take the man out of the Dominican Republic, he allegedly told her, but you can't take it out of the man.

The poet Shreerekha Subramanian, an associate professor of humanities at the University of Houston at Clear Lake, also outed herself as the lover "S" in Díaz's *New Yorker* piece, saying (without naming Díaz explicitly) that he swore her to silence during their relationship, when she was a graduate student at Rutgers

University. She said he loved her because she identified as Black, but eventually dumped her because she wasn't Black enough (Subramanian is of South Asian descent). (From *Inside Education*, May 28, 2018.)

Another honorary feminist, Robert Elliot Fox, made a scene at a party that Professor Werner Sollors held for me when I was a visiting Professor at Harvard in 1989. He accosted me about my misogyny. I asked him about the treatment of Polish women by Polish men. Fox is the go-to guy when other critics want to do a quick and lazy Cliff Notes review of my books instead of reading them. He wrote *Conscientious Sorcerers: The Black Postmodernist Fiction of LeRoi Jones/Amiri Baraka, Ishmael Reed, and Samuel R. Delany,* but has given no evidence that he has kept up with my work since the book's publication in 1987. He once called me paranoid, which means that the lenses through which he perceives reality are superior to mine.

He gets his lenses at Tiffany's. I get mine at Target.

A Polish American, he said he didn't identify as a Pole. He later confessed that he was only trying to score Brownie Points with feminists by attacking me. He said he was upset by how Nigerian men were treating Nigerian women—he married a Nigerian woman—but takes no stand on how Polish women are treated?

I had an exchange with Caitlin Flanagan, who wrote about how mean Black men treat Black women. I asked her whether Irish-American men should write a manual about the treatment of women that Black men could follow. An Italian American scholar criticized my views about *Precious*, a film worse than *Birth of a Nation*.

Maverick critic Armond White agreed. Maybe Italian American men might co-write that manual.

Filmmaker Pratibha Parmar, (*Alice Walker: Beauty in Truth* (2013) cited me in this PBS documentary as someone who was opposed to Steven Spielberg's interpretation of Black male culture in *The Color Purple*, and indicted both Black men and women for their criticism of the film. I tried to engage in a dialogue with her. She never responded to my emails. She is an Indian woman. India has the largest number of enslaved in the world, over 11 million, most of them women and girls. No film from her about that? Like Parmar, *Times* writer Parul Sehgal also admires books in which Black men are depicted as rapists. Rape is rampant in India. She should join the Indian feminists who challenge a stern patriarchy as well as Black male rapists. I read works by Indian women for my novel, *Conjugating Hindi*. They complain that they are slaves of their fathers, sons and mothers-in-law.

While Pratibha Parmar avoided me, to her credit Parul Sehgal, a writer for the *Times* responded to my questions. She said she had criticized misogyny in India and in her own family. But why didn't Pratibha Parmar and Parul Sehgal criticize Spielberg's *Raiders of the Lost Ark*, which insulted Hinduism and the goddess Kali? He was accused of erasing Chinese culture in *Kingdom of the Sun*, which he directed. Critics observed that the film "oddly erases the Chinese from a story in China, relegating them to background roles like chauffeurs, gardeners, nannies, and beggars, who are largely 'nameless throngs.' The main narrative focuses on the experiences of the privileged British boy, Jim Graham, and other Western characters and Japanese captors."

Writing in *The San Jose Mercury News* in December 1986, Irish American writer Jack Foley accused Spielberg of defaming the Irish in *American Tail* under the headline, "Spielberg Film Promotes Prejudice Against The Irish." He wrote, "Spielberg has a real character flaw when it comes to ethnic types, offending some Asians with *Indiana Jones and the Temple of Doom* and some Blacks with *The Color Purple*." Like feminists from other ethnic groups, feminists like Pratibha Parmar and Parul Sehgal find it easier to critique Black male chauvinism than that practiced by men who belong to their ethnic groups. Some Indian women who have criticized the Indian patriarchy have had to go into hiding though Durba Mitra writes, in *Indian Sex Life: Sexuality and the Colonial Origins of Modern Social Thought*, that it was outsiders, English and German men using old texts, who defined Indian gender relations. Something like that is happening here which is why Morrison says the conflict between Black writers is being promoted by outsiders.

Another honorary Black feminist critic, Gerald Nicosia, who received an advance from St. Martin's to write a biography of Ntozake Shange, said that Amiri Baraka and I opposed Shange's work. Ntozake Shange's family called out the lie perpetrated by this honorary Black feminist, and *The Washington Post* apologized to me. Probably the first time *The Washington Post* apologized to a Black.

I was in contact with Ntozake weekly before her death and was the first to publish an excerpt from *For Colored Girls Who Have Considered Suicide/ When the*

Rainbow is Enuf, in 1984. When some white feminists in San Francisco asked her to condemn me, she refused.

When Spielberg read *The Color Purple*, he said all he could think about was "rescuing Celie." What about rescuing Naomi and Rachel? In *The Tablet*, a Jewish magazine, I challenged him to make a film about the oppression of Jewish women by Jewish men in the United States and Israel. When I visited Israel, feminists were demonstrating before the Knesset over the murder of Israeli women by Israeli men. The magazine *Lillith* reports that domestic violence against American Jewish women has been covered up. I wonder will *Times* writer Sasha Weiss ever write about this cover up?

Maybe David Zirin didn't know this when he came out as a Black feminist. We were supposed to appear on Amy Goodman's show to talk about my book, *The Complete Muhammad Ali*. I was interviewed by a *Democracy Now* staff member before the show aired. I told her that I would ask Zirin, the honorary Black feminist, about the treatment of Jewish women in the United States and abroad. When asked to join the Black feminists, he was a no-show.

As early as the 1970s, Barbara Smith in her article "Toward a Black Feminist Criticism" labeled me the nation's "notorious misogynist writer... in perfect agreement with the values of a society that hates the black people, women, and black women." Smith found support from Andrew Strombeck in his 2006 thesis "The Conspiracy of Masculinity in Ishmael Reed," which pointed out "the masculine unconscious at work in *Mumbo Jumbo* (1972) and *Reckless Eyeballing* (1986)."

Strombeck is a German American, one of many men from other ethnic groups who've signed on as honorary Black feminists. When she attacked me in Ms. about a novel she gave no evidence as having read, Ms. was owned by men, Lang Communications.

As mentioned above, Harriet Fraad believes Gloria Steinem co-opted a movement that began as working class and integrated. She and others have brought up Steinem's ties to the CIA.[1] What could be more beneficial to those who've been hostile to the dissent posed by Black male writers historically than to put them on the defensive with charges of misogyny? Not that they can't be stupid about women. I've been there, and I've found that most of the Blues written by Black men are whiny about how they've been mistreated by women. They're not the only American crybabies and Mama's boys. The media is feeling sorry for young white men who are depressed about their condition in American society, when they're the most privileged group in the history of the species. For them, Donald Trump, a demented clown, who has been convicted of sexual aggression, and is a possible pedophile and a convicted felon, is an example of manhood. Some of them are so frustrated with their lot that they support Nick Fuentes, who says he wants a Nazi candidate for president. Despite this announcement, Vice President Vance says that there's room in the Republican Party for him. All you have to

1. Josh Jones, "How the CIA Funded & Supported Literary Magazines Worldwide While Waging Cultural War Against Communism," *Open Culture*, 27 October 2017.

know about Vance is that when his mother was in desperate need of help, he turned her down.

The Village Voice also printed James Baldwin's lie that I called him a "cocksucker" every time I encountered him. As has been the case with other magazines where I have been lied about, nobody fact-checked this lie with me. The New York Literary Establishment broke ties with Baldwin after he mercilessly satirized Lee Strasberg for the Actors Studio's handling of his play, *Blues for Mr. Charlie*. Mario Puzo was chosen to do a hatchet job on Baldwin's best novel, *Tell Me How Long the Train's Been Gone*, in *The New York Times*. After his insult to a member of "The Family," an aggregate of Manhattan literary powers, Baldwin was replaced by Eldridge Cleaver, whose feud with the Black Panther Party helped to destroy the party.

In our magazine *Yardbird Reader*, Al Young and I printed an interview with Truman Capote, conducted by writer Cecil Brown. He said that The Family was treating Baldwin like "shit." I was instrumental in securing Baldwin a Regent's lectureship at the University of California at Berkeley and, later, a job at Bowling Green State University through my friend, the poet Howard McCord. Since Baldwin's comment that I called him a "cocksucker," mentally unstable people have given me problems. The most recent Baldwin fan who excoriated me in a Seattle magazine admitted that he was "suicidal." I tried to reach out to this critic. I invited him to contribute to my magazine, *Konch*. He answered, he'd rather be dead than me. If he does commit suicide, would I be guilty of assisted suicide?

Village Voice feminists were among those who created the atmosphere that led to the conviction of the Central Park Five, but when writer Rivka Gerwirtz Little ("Rage Before Race," *Village Voice*, Oct.15, 2002) asked for comments after another person was found responsible for the crime, she said that few of the feminists who had prejudged the CP5 answered her phone calls.

Journalist Margo Jefferson has been so furious about my work that she made a scene at a party I held to celebrate the publication of Calvin Hernton's poetry book, *Medicine Man*. Before an audience at New York University, she threatened me with physical assault. The women in the audience applauded. Yet she called John Wayne, a racist and sexist, "Handsome and beautiful," and said that she had erotic fantasies about him.

Why do I call out these hypocrisies? The mission of the Haitian loa of satire, Guede, and his Yoruba antecedent Iku, is to show each man (and woman) their devils. These women who claim they're opposed to battery applaud the possible battery of a man? I showed them their devil that day.

So the idea arose in the late seventies that Black women writers had eclipsed Black male writers, which is how it was put by a white feminist, then an aide to Senator Robert Dole, who interviewed me on a radio show in the 1970s. Concomitant with the effort to drive Black male writers was the rise of Black Boogeyman literature, especially with the theme of incest. Black Bogeyman literature has enriched both Black and white women, such as writers like Katherine Stockett who wrote *The Help*.

A Black domestic said that the lead character in the book was based on her and sued. None of the white men belong to the White Citizens' Council or the Klan. One white man slaps a Black woman who steals an item from her employer. But he's an underclass cop. White trash. The middle-class white men are benign. One even helps a Black woman with her groceries, and a Black villain is Leroy, who beats his wife. The film takes place during the time of the Medgar Evers killing. Mississippi-born Tate Tayor wrote the script and directed the film.

In a *New York Times*' review of Toni Morrison's *The Bluest Eye*, in which a Black father rapes his daughter on the kitchen floor, Diane Johnson wrote that the "largely white audience thrills voyeuristically to the Black incest literature. We press our noses to the window to see the black mama suckling her school-age son, the black papa committing incest." "The Song of Toni Morrison" by Colette Dowling, *The New York Times*, May 20, 1979. This explains why some critics praised Ellison's *The Invisible Man,* not for the lofty intellectual debates, but for Trueblood, the farmer who has sex with his daughter.

Jesmyn Ward said that she was inspired by Morrison and Walker's treatment of incest. She was writing on behalf of the National Book Foundation, whose president belongs to a group whose men have been libeled as incest perpetrators for centuries.

Though the authors of Black incest novels were found marketable, white men made most of the money from such products. *Precious* is the worst movie about Black life ever made. In this evil thing, both the Black father and mother engage in incest. *Precious* was produced by a woman whose ethnic group has also been subjected to such pernicious slander for centuries. The film was based on a book by Sapphire.

Sapphire was one of those who prejudged the Central Park 5. She wrote a poem called "Wild Thing" which placed the Central Park Five at the scene of the rape.

Let's get a female jogger!
I shout into the twilight
looking at the
middle-class thighs
pumping past me,
cadres of bitches
who deserve to die
for thinking they're better
than me
You ain't better than
nobody bitch.
The rock begs my hand
to hold it.
It says, "Come on man."
T.W., Pit Bull, J.D. & me
grab the bitch
ugly big nose white bitch
but she's beautiful cause she's white
she's beautiful cause she's skinny
she's beautiful couse she's gonna die
cause her daddy's gonna cry
Bitch!
I bring the rock down
on her head

Darryl Pinckney has shown that writing Black incest novels for profit is nothing new. He cites a book by a white author who received the Pulitzer Prize. She wrote a novel about a Black man who marries his daughter.

The brawl over my novel *Reckless Eyeballing* and the snuff job that feminists at *The Times* did on *The Terrible Threes* and *Reckless Eyeballing,* led me to become a global writer. I vowed that never again would I be subjected to the literary drubbing from narrow, faux Eurocentric critics and their collaborators. (Faux because though there are fifty-five countries in Europe, most Americans view Europe as having something to do with Buckingham Palace.)

After the critical sabotage of *Reckless Eyeballing* and *The Terrible Threes,* my enemies considered me a literary roadkill.

My breakthrough came when I studied Japanese and wrote *Japanese by Spring.* It was published by Putnam in 1995. It's still in print. This earned me trips to Japan and China, where the novel was adopted as a National Project, meaning the government funded research on it. On one trip, "Conjure," a band that's been playing songs composed by leading composers, using my poetry as lyrics, performed at the Blue Note in Tokyo while I read a song I'd written in Japanese. I couldn't get beyond the second line before there was applause from the audience.

Unlike the flip, ignorant dismissals of *Juice!* by critics in this country, a young professor, the late Yuqing Lin, wrote a thorough review of the novel. She came to Berkeley for a year to study my work.

My study of Hindi, which I applied to my novel *Conjugating Hindi*, published by Dalkey Archives, was way above the pay grade of the average Eurocentric critic and their kitchen help. I adapted the novel for the stage in a two-act play, entitled *The Conductor*, about a Black man who runs an underground railroad on behalf of Indians who are fleeing the USA after an Indian dictator has put heat on them.

My study of Hindi enabled me to hire two actors of South Asian ancestry to perform in *The Conductor*. My study of Yoruba prepared me to present a work I wrote in Yoruba before an audience in Lagos. After leaving Nigeria, I published two books by Nigerian authors, including *16 Short Stories by Nigerian Women*. I sold both to the Egyptian Center for Translation, which translated the books into Arabic. So my becoming a global author freed me from American critics like Paul Devlin, who said that I have gone "too far," the kind of instructions made to fugitive slave Henry Bibb from his former slave owner. (Bibb told him where to go and what to do with himself.)

Quebec publisher Robin Philpot published *The Terrible Fours* and has published *The Terrible Fives*. *The Terribles* series has earned their titles as prophetic books. *The Terrible Twos* (1982) predicted the fall of the Soviet Union and the city where the revolt would begin: Riga, Latvia.

William Gates, the CIA director at the time, said he was surprised by the Soviet Union's unravelling.

The Terrible Threes (1989) predicted the arrival of a fascist dictatorship. *The Terrible Fours* predicted the entrance of a Black Pope.

And *The Terrible Fives*? Read and find out. Some uncanny events have occurred during my writing career.

The Terrible Fives, being published by a Canadian publisher during the same year as the publication of the 50th anniversary edition of *Flight to Canada* is one of those. And the final irony, Random House, which thought *Flight to Canada* too experimental, is distributing my introduction to William Demby's *Love Story Black*, a novel that I published after Random House rejected it. For not being commercial enough.

The Terrible Fives

CHAPTER 1

The Terrible Threes, completed in 1988, and published in 1989, includes the following passage:

> The D'Roaches, a derisive term given the Amerikander Party led by a forty-year-old skinhead named Termite Control, was gaining in the polls, but all of the pundits agreed that this party, which was on the ballot in twelve states, didn't have a chance. The American people weren't that gullible. Jesse Hatch and Reverend Jones called for national unity and promised that the kidnappers of former president Dean Clift would be brought to justice. Tonight, Xmas Night, Reverend Jones would lead the nation in prayer for the recovery from The Terribles, which have plagued the nation since Dallas, Nov. 22, 1963.
>
> Oakland, California, November 7, 1988

Luke Lockett, aka Termite Control, (based upon General Westmoreland's referring to the Vietnamese as "termites,") was dedicated to 18th century values, when Blacks and Indians were slaves and a woman's uterus was the property of men. He campaigned for an Antebellum Restoration trend. But given their white trash origins, in the 19th Century, the D'Roaches would be patrollers instead of plantation owners. Patrollers were the poor saps who believed that their fate, as whites, somehow linked them to the white planters or Anglo Saxons as they called themselves. Laboring under propaganda that convinced them that the status of Blacks at the bottom made them aristocrats, thousands were killed on behalf of a South in which they were yeomen. Though Termite and his followers worship the Nørse god Odin, millions of them are of Mediterranean origin, or from places like the Balkans, yet Termite promises that if elected he will tear down the statute of Thomas Jefferson, in Termite's opinion a wishy-washy Deist, and replace it with a golden statue of Odin. For some Nordic purists the standards for white Supermen had become so low that even a dark skinned Indian man,who would be considered an untouchable were he in India can tell somebody that he'd meet them in Vallhallah.

At the end of *The Terrible Fours* (2021), not only is Termite Control, the Necrophiliac, introduced in *The Terrible Threes* (1989), gaining in the polls but he now has a chance of winning the election because of a scandal that has rocked the nation. Considered a joke and his movement dismissed as a clown car in a bankrupt circus, none gave Termite Control a chance to unseat the Hatch regime, which had gotten their Rapture congress people to eliminate the 22nd Amendment limiting the president to two terms. But now, Termite was no longer funny.

Hobbomock, the *Quinnipiac* trickster, was angry with Rev. Clement Jones, chief of staff to President Jesse Hatch. Hobbomock introduced in *The Terrible Fours*, had disarmed the Devil who had interrupted former president Dean Clift's triumphant return to Washington after Supreme Court Justice Nola Payne had cast the vote declaring his ouster, led by Rev. Clement Jones, to be unconstitutional.

Jones gave the Devil a lease on his Essence in exchange for the Devil's deed. A quid pro quo. But the lease which was supposed to be renewed each year had expired because the Devil, whose career is that of a loser, forgot the date of renewal, which was the day before the Devil, Clement Jones, and Hobbomock met in the Oval Office where the Devil was to inform Jones that his Essence now belonged to a pagan entity. The Devil was having such a good time on the way to D.C., he had forgotten the date. Jones thought the whole episode funny. Hobbomock swore that he would get even with Jones for the insult. He found an opportunity.

JFK, Jr. shows President Hatch how to handle blackmail.

Author joins QAnon buddies as we await JFK's arrival in Dallas.

Hobbomock is a shape shifter who at the end of *The Terrible Fours*, disguised as JFK Jr., visited President Hatch at Camp David after Rev. Jones had ridiculed Jesse Hatch at a private party held at the camp David in his usual most sadistic manner, leaving some of the guests rolling in the aisles with laughter at the expense of Hatch.

It all began when JFK Jr. abandoned his trip to Dallas where crowds of adoring QAnon fans were expecting him, and his father, JFK, and visited President Hatch, who was weeping in a cabin at Camp David after another humiliation by Chief-of-Staff Rev. Clement Jones. Hobbomock can appear as a deer, a man, or an eagle, but his favorite forms are the eel and the snake. Terrifyingly, Hobbomock also sometimes appears as a European, as John Josselyn recorded in 1674. And this is how he chose to present himself most of the time in *The Terribles* series. As a white man. He is only six feet tall, instead of being a giant, which got him into trouble. Upset that his people no longer revered him, his wrath took a heavy handed form. He stamped his foot, changing the course of the Connecticut River. This gave his enemies an opening. So Kiehtan, a benevolent creator god, or in the eyes of the invaders "a good Indian" cast a spell on Hobbomock which put him in "deep slumber."

Another version has Hobbomock's slumber the result of eating too many oysters. This slumber period gave him time to think of a new way to achieve his goal, that of saving the beauty of the land and protecting the earth's animals, thousands of which were becoming extinct as a result of human practices. And so when he escaped from Sleeping Mountain because the spell wore off, Hobbomock tried a new tactic. He got wind of the Devil's agreement with Chief-of-Staff Rev. Clement Jones. He planned to make the Devil his captive and hand Jones's Essence over to him. That way he could control Jones and use his power to promote green energy.

Jesse Hatch was touched that JFK Jr. (Hobbomock disguised as a white man) had interrupted his trip to Dallas. And here he was consoling him. JFK Jr. told Hatch what he must do. Come out. Go public with the secret that Rev. Jones held over him. The one that made him powerless and a human rug that the Rev. could wipe his muddy boot on. No longer would he be blackmailed. The *Quinnipiac* trickster who is capable of "divers shapes" was both JFK Jr. and Carolyn Bessette-Kennedy. Hobbomock was still smarting over Rev. Clement Jones laughing at him and the Devil in the Oval Office.

Chapter 2

Persuaded by JFK Jr. (Hobbomock), President Hatch decided to reveal the secret that Chief-of-Staff held over him. He called a press conference.

Hatch was standing behind a lectern. In front was the presidential seal. Hatch was wearing a dress, high heels, maybe a little too much rouge. His speech began: "I was born with interchangeable genitalia. I'm a quadruple binary," he said.

Some reporters rushed from the press room after hearing this announcement that "Only Rev. Clement Jones and my ex-wife know my secret." And he could have also mentioned his favorite prostitute, Holly, whose Madame ran the House of Minerva, where sex workers fulfilled his complex sexual desires and those of other politicians. Hatch explained: "I can no longer carry this burden. That's why I'm coming out. Rev. Clement Jones has been blackmailing me for years. It was Rev. Jones who was behind the murder of Admiral Matthews because the Admiral was about to reveal Operation Two Birds, a plan by Rev. Clement Jones, under the suggestion of his then mentor Rev. Sunshine Mooney, that New York, the Babylon of the Bible, be bombed. The bombing would be blamed on an African nation that was developing a bomb. It was called Operation Two Birds. (By the end of 2025, the African continent had successfully launched 68 satellites.)

Hatch continued: "I also suggest that a grand jury be impaneled to investigate the suicide of the Secretary of State and the murder of the Secretary of Defense. Clement's overseas travels were merely excuses for him to collect bribes. He's taken millions in bribes. He's taken millions. With his investments in crypto-currency, millions more will go into his pocket and those of his friends."

Finally, what newspapers call a bombshell happened. During the press conference that Hatch called, he turned the microphone over to a young man who was standing beside him. The young man told the assembled press that Clement Jones had paid him money to kill his mother so that she couldn't challenge his inheritance of his late father's empire. Jones had failed to get her to award him power of attorney over her.

Rev. Jones's mother was a patient in a nursing home where he worked as an orderly. The young man said he told Rev. Jones that he'd done the deed and buried her. This was a lie. Realizing that Clement Jones's mother was in danger, the orderly had set up living quarters for the woman in the basement of his house. She was willing to testify against her son. The orderly said he had a recording of Clement Jones asking him to commit the foul deed.

To think Rev. Jones had begun as a bohemian and as a protester. He even had an apartment in Greenwich

Village. Smoked pot. Dated Black and Puerto Rican women. Taught for twenty years at Queens College. Spent a lot of time packing and unpacking ideas. Like many Manhattan intellectuals, he waited patiently for the latest theories from France or Germany that he could copy, and worked on his British accent, but then one of the deacons of his father's church asked whether he wanted to spend the rest of his life grading papers or gain power and make some money. That persuaded him. This wouldn't be the first time that a progressive turned right. Socialist Max Eastman ended his career writing for *The National Review.*

The President left the press room without taking questions. But not before turning the questions over to the new acting Attorney General, who issued an arrest warrant for Jones and the Rapture Attorney General whom he replaced. For years the Rapture Attorney General had jailed members of the press and others whom the Jones government considered enemies. Andrew Jackson would be proud because this is how he operated. He censored pro-abolitionist literature from being circulated in the South.

Rev. Clement Jones was addressing the National Prayer Breakfast which was taking place in the International Ballroom of the Washington Hilton Hotel. Fundamentalist Christian nationalist preachers from all over the country had arrived in Washington for the annual event. Rev. Sunshine Mooney introduced him. Some of the members of his delegation had embarrassed the Rev. The night before, the reverends had an orgy in one of the downtown hotels. The prostitutes were arrested as they tried to exit the hotel with their money and credit cards, but the White House intervened as a favor to Rev. Mooney who had thrown the support of his millions of followers to the Hatch administration. Sunshine Mooney introduced Jones. He received a standing ovation. He made a few jokes as a warmup, mostly at the expense of President Hatch. He was winding up:

"... And then the asshole comes into the state dinner, like you had all of these foreign dignitaries attending the event that honored one of these rug salesmen, some sheik, and Hatch is wearing mixed matched socks, and when introduced the son of a bitch had fallen asleep."

After the laughter died down, Jones became serious. "Fellows in Christ, those who ridiculed our version of the End Times, with the Ascension of Bob Krantz, praise the Lord, Hallelujah, the return of the Messiah is imminent, Praise the Lord, Hallelujah." He received another standing ovation. People began waving their arms, their eyes closed, looking toward heaven. Rev. Jones's eyes went to the back of his head. He started speaking in tongues. He leaped from the dais and began doing the holiness dance. Others joined in. This white preacher was to evangelism like Elvis Presley was to Rock and Roll. He'd studied Black preachers like Rev. Franklin, and Rev. Ike whose Religion of Prosperity he'd copied. After the dance of holiness, he jumped back to the dais.

"Now, our church was in trouble until this Ascension. People were becoming skeptical. Pagan forces were rising. Like Termite Control, a man who sleeps with dead women. Worships a Viking god Odin. Surrounds himself with a group of paramilitary thugs whom we call D'Roaches. This creep thinks he has a chance of winning the presidency with a lot of fake promises. Like he wants to protect the border. We did that. These wetbacks know better than to rent our borders and we've seen to it that their asses are sent back to the shithole countries of their origin." Another standing ovation. "Now a lot of you are getting impatient. We get tons of mail each day. Citizens wanting to know, when am I going to get my Ascension? When is the Lord going to call me home? Some of you in this room have questions. All I have to say is you can't rush Jeeeeeeeesus." Sunshine Mooney got to his feet. Addressing the audience, he said, "Amen! Jesus' timetable ain't got nuthin to do with you. You just going to have to wait. Get in line and have patience, praise the Lord, Hallelujah."

Mooney continued his address: "Now Termite says he wants to build a golden statue of Odin, a Viking god where the Washington monument now stands. Says he wants to remind white Americans of their glorious past. We going to let him do that?" Somebody in the audience said "Hell no." A woman jumped up and started banging on a tambourine. Her dancing started some of the others running up and down the aisle. The organist began to play along with the dancing. Rev. Mooney and some of the other ministers on the dais got up and did their steps. When it all died down, Rev. Jones, the most powerful man in the West, was sweating. "Who does Termite remind you of?" Rev. Jones asked. He cupped his ear. No answer from the congregation. So Jones continued:

Nebuchadnezzar. He also built a big old image of gold, whose height was threescore cubits, and the breadth thereof six cubits: He summoned all of the princes, the governors, and the captains, the judges, the treasurers, the counsellors, the sheriffs, and all the rulers of the provinces, to come to the dedication of the image which Nebuchadnezzar the king had set up. And one of the worshippers told the King there are Jews who say they not going to worship your golden idol. They are Shadrach, Meshach, and Abednego. They serve not thy gods, nor worship the golden image which thou hast set. And before you knowed it, the king was eating grass like an oxen and baying like an ass.

None of the usual amens followed this declaration.

There was silence. People in the audience were looking at their phones. So were those who were seated on the dais. Puzzled, Rev. Jones looked at Rev. Mooney. Mooney stood up and showed him the message on the phone. President Hatch had had a press conference and revealed the secret with which Jones had blackmailed him. Not only that, he'd listed the crimes that Jones had committed. A warrant for Jones' arrest had been issued. Shocked, Mooney stared at Jones. The ministers who shared the dais where Jones and Mooney were seated were alarmed and confused. Hearing sirens, Rev. Jones took off through the doors of the room in which the prayer service was being held, startling the cooks as he ran through the hotel kitchen and into an alley, knocking over garbage cans. He headed into the Washington streets, just as the police were pulling up to the Hilton, and got lost in the passing crowds.

Termite Control was about to be interviewed on a daytime TV talk show. Someone handed the talk show host a note. He read it and then addressed the audience. "Ladies and Gentlemen, while we've been on the air, President Hatch had a news conference in which he revealed himself to be a quadruple binary. He accused his Chief of Staff Rev. Clement Jones of murder." There was much commotion in the audience and quite a few gasps. The host called for silence. He kept reading: "Rev. Jones was addressing the National Prayer breakfast and when informed of President Hatch's press conference, Rev. Jones fled the prayer breakfast. This will lead to an opening for Termite Control and candidates of the Amerikaner party, men and women who worship the Viking god Odin. Nobody had given them a chance, but now they have a clear path to win the election, resulting from Rev. Jones being on the run and—" The host paused. "More fast-moving events ladies and gentlemen. Will President Hatch negotiate a plea deal with the Attorney General? With these developments, will their critics continue to dismiss Termite's followers as D'Roaches? Nothing funny anymore. There are only a few months before election day, and within an hour of the possible fall of the Hatch government Las Vegas money will probably have Termite as a shoo-in. Termite's only opposition in the election is Kingsley Scab, or Scabb, the former Vice President and Bruce Cream, the father of a white Hip Hop star Ice Cream, who'd murdered a Black intruder who knocked on his door in a stand-your-ground incident. (Actually, the intruder was his son, Ice Cream, who thought that it would be fun to show up to an awards ceremony in Blackface, but couldn't remove it. He was being pursued by police for murdering himself. Thought he'd be safe at his parents' home, but because of his Blackface, his dad mistook him for a home invader and shot him through the door, becoming a hero to millions and raising ten million dollars for a defense fund.)"

The moderator of the daytime show looked into the camera. Heralding Termite Control as a breath of fresh air, the moderator introduced Termite Control. As he walked onto the set from the Green Room where he'd been reading *Eric the Red's Saga*, Termite was met by screams and feet stomping from the women in the audience. This was noticed by the interviewer.

"Ladies and Gentlemen, we are pleased to have as our guest Luke Lockett, a.k.a. Termite Control. He claims to be a direct descendant of the Viking hero Eric the Red, but before we begin to talk about his presidential campaign, I want to ask you Luke about events that have happened during the last two hours. The Chief of Staff Jones has fled the prayer breakfast after President Hatch called him a murderer."

Termite: "This is what happens when an administration stays in office too long. The scandals accumulate. It's also another blow to Christianity, a religion of the weak and the soft. This is why church attendance in this country has plummeted." Luke read from a sheet: "U.S. church membership has fallen below 50%, with significant, long-term declines in attendance driven by a rise in the 'nones' unaffiliated, generational shifts especially among Millennials/Gen Z, and, more recently, the impact of the COVID-19 pandemic. Weekly attendance has dropped from over 40% two decades ago to around 30%. People want something new, especially young men. We Vikings will provide them with an alternative. Our poll numbers are bound to shoot up now that President Hatch has turned the tables on Rev. Jones. You have to hand it to Hatch. I guess he got tired of being a butt of jokes by Jones. He never missed a chance to clown Hatch. Turns out that Hatch has balls after all."

INT: "He turned up at the press conference wearing a dress."
TC: "What?" There was laughter from the audience. "Further proof that the country has a manhood crisis. Our people worship a warrior god, Odin. We plan to tear down the Washington Monument and replace it with a golden statue of Odin. Remind white people of their Viking heritage."

Many whites stood and applauded. Other whites and Blacks and Browns kept their seats.

INT: "Does this means that they're not going to get rid of their horned helmets, bear skin attire, and beards. No more bonfires?"
TC: "Not on your life. We will maintain our costumes and rituals. The date of the Winter Solstice will be a national holiday."
INT: "If men start wearing bear skin and helmets, instead of suits and hats, won't that put the fashion industry out of business?"

TC: "Who cares, the fashion industry is dominated by queers."

There were some boos. Two of Termite's D'Roaches roughly threw the offenders out of the auditorium to the applause of the audience.

INT: "And are you sure that the American public is ready to elect a man who -"
TC: "Sleeps with dead women?"
INT: "A Necrophiliac?"
TC: "Necrophilia is sweeping Europe. The youth branch of the Swedish Liberal People's Party is advocating that Necrophilia be legalized. They argue that people should get to decide what happens to their bodies after they die, and not the Deep State. No one objects to someone who wants to bequeath their body to science, and what's wrong with someone donating their body for another person's pleasure? Isn't it bad enough that the Deep State determines what you should do with your body when you're alive, but then they have control over what you do with your body after death?"
INT: "But most people find such practices that you advocate are disgusting."
TC: "We operate on a three-day rule."
INT: "Meaning?"
TC: "No sex with a dear departed one after three days following their death."
INT: "Tell us about the rally."
TC: "Our next campaign rally will be launched next week. Thousands of Necrophiliacs are expected to attend."

INT: "There were demonstrators greeting you as you entered the building. If you are elected, how will you handle them?"
TC. "If they demonstrate against me, they'd better leave a note with their kin indicating where their remains should be sent. And if anyone throws a missive at my police and my soldiers that will be the last missive they throw."
INT: "That's coming on pretty strong, don't you think? What about Constitutional rights?"
TC: "Those who are poisoning the blood of our citizens have to be dealt with. You have the mentally ill invading our country. Other countries are emptying their prisons and sending them here. And one more thing. We will abandon English, which is no match for Spanish, a language that you can dance to. We will insist that our language will be that of our mother tongue. Norse. I carry Norse dictionaries with me. My assistants have distributed copies to members of the audience. We must recover our mother tongue. The English language is a whore. It absorbs parts of speech from barbaric languages. Norse is our pure uncorrupted white language."
INT. "Thank you Termite. Termite Control, everybody."
TC: "Ekki at Pakka, That's Norse for think nothing of it."

Termite exited the stage to thunderous applause. Termite waved to the audience as he exited the stage, but when he exited from the building he was greeted by boos and signs that ridiculed his way of love making.

Some audience members were wearing caps and T-shirts on which were printed pictures of Termite's spray can. Instead of condemning a situation where a Necrophiliac could become president of the United States, during the panel discussion held after the interview, liberal columnists for *The New York Record* made excuses for the followers of Termite Control, who threatened to close the borders and expel American-born citizens no matter how many generations of their ancestors had dwelled here. He'd promised that those among his followers, who'd been agitating (since the T.2's) that Hitler's birthday be recognized and MLK's be dropped, would get their wish. MLK's notorious hotel tape was used as an excuse to dishonor King. Termite said that under his administration all of the Confederate statues that had been taken down, would be put back up.

INT: "For years, people had dismissed the Amerikaner party as a place where the Odin cult mobilized men who gained pounds while living in the basements of their parents' homes, staring at reels on Facebook and thumbing through social media all day while subsisting on Slurpees. Not anymore. They're being taken seriously now. They've even adopted the name their enemies gave them. D'Roaches. Termite Control gives hope to those who have lost hope. Thank you, Luke Lockett, a.k.a. Termite Control."

Following the interview, panelists discussed what Termite had said. The question was why a man who admits to sleeping with dead women was gaining in the polls and, now that the Clement/Hatch administration had collapsed, had a clear path to the presidency. A plump Black woman with big cheeks led the discussion. "I think the country is at a tipping point. A man who sleeps with dead people might become president."

She was answered by a panelist. "But Termite has moderated his views, don't you think? He says that he and his followers have a three-day rule. No sleeping with the dead three days after their death. And he makes a point: Some people sign their cadavers over to medical research. What's wrong with someone signing their cadaver to be used for pleasure?"

Another one said: "He's promised to get rid of that robot who goes around beating up people and the ghost of the SS soldier, the one who stowed away on Reagan's Air Force One on his return from laying a wreath at the grave of the Nazi dead at Bitburg."

Five-year-old Chelsea Clinton had written, *"Dear Mr. President, I have seen the Sound of Music. The Nazi don't look very nice people. Please don't go to their cemetery."*

One columnist blamed the rise of Termite on what he called the Brahman Left, always protesting whatever. He wrote, this only alienates the Reagan coalition of the 1980s, whose resentments and grievances have been ignored. They're also losing among Black, Latino, and Asian American working-class voters. He said that Termite Control is the perfect vehicle for their anger. The columnist's argument held the elites, of which he was a member, responsible for the popularity of Termite Control, who promised to spray their enemies. Another columnist who had a bug up his ass about Black people blamed Termite's ascendency on the culture of white

Americans being replaced, which was a dog whistle about Hip Hop.

The moderator asked, "Could any fiction writer make up what happened today? The coming out of Jesse Hatch. The search for Rev. Jones, wanted for murder."

Another panelist chimed in. "Now that Rev. Jones has been exposed as a corrupt criminal who enticed his followers into believing that the Rapture had begun because one of his advisors, Bob Krantz, had ascended, which was probably fake.

Another Yale-educated panelist blamed the support for Termite on the unraveling of American morality that occurred during the 1960s. As for Necrophilia, he said, "we had an administration where every other member including the president was fucking 10 and 12 year olds. Which is worse, pedophilia, or necrophilia? Which is more harmful?" His fellow panelists nodded in agreement.

Later, Termite and his campaign workers were watching a tape of the interview from his headquarters. Giving one another the hi-five over his performance. His chief aides, Gut Bomb, Cyclo Spora and Meso Thelioma, were knocking down some strong whiskey, hugging each other and slapping each other on the butt.

Now the front runner for the presidency, Termite leaned back in his chair with his hands cupping his head. To think, nobody thought that he had a chance and now he'd become the front runner. The perks—a billionaire with ties to other AI billionaires had called. Offered to lend him a plane that was as big as Air Force One. He was being courted by lobbyists, and the most important, in his eyes, were the lobbyists for morticians. *Business Insider* said their industry was suffering from "Rising costs, declining demand, and government scrutiny." More people were choosing cremation.

"Their historic business of preserving a body, displaying, it and then overseeing its burial is collapsing." The morticians had instructed Termite that, as far as they were concerned, all D.C. mortuaries were open houses for Termite, no matter how late at night. He'd have to promise to end cremation. But hey, he'd only run for president to sell Termite spray cans which the suckers bought in millions, and now he was the front runner, his only competition being former vice president Scab and the father of the white rap star Ice Cream, Bruce Cream. He would need a communications director. That's where Vixen came in.

Chapter 3

Vixen Gritt (T.2's), a stout red head, had a good education and more options available to her than her Black, Brown, Yellow and Native American sisters. The murder of Native American women by white men isn't even noticed by the media. After college, Vixen lived with a talentless painter named Sam. They broke up, and last time she saw him, he was driving a cab. Like many painters, he'd been liquidated by the billion-dollar Warhol machine, which declared anything you found in the grocery store was art and that painting was dead.

Sam never found out that she was sleeping with his best friend, Romero, the only one of her lovers who took his time. She was in love with Romero, but he had two disabled children and a mentally ill wife. He was chained to a boring, contentious marriage. He never knew when his wife, Sylvia, would have one of her psychotic episodes. During one, she accused him of poisoning her. Then she started fucking all of his friends. He'd come home from working in an arts supply store and found that she'd taken the scissors to his clothing. Or that she'd forgotten to pick up the children from school. Vixen detached herself from what was a gothic situation.

Finally, Vixen, like others, was stirred by the Christmas riot that took place at the annual Madison Square Garden Christmas festivities, when Santa Claus disrupted the celebration by making an anarchist speech and insulting the VIPs with whom he shared the dais. At that time, she was sympathetic to anarchism. Little did she know that this Santa Claus was the body of a white gangster named Snowman. This Santa Claus was a member of The Walking Dead. Manipulated and ventriloquized by an impish vertically challenged Black man. He was a sinister fake Rasta man who went by the name of Black Peter. Black Peter had taken over Snowman's mouth.

You see: two losers, inept and aging Black pimps, Joe Baby and Big Meat, had hired a white hitman named Snowman to kill Boy Bishop, who had rescued two of their prostitutes, Barbara and Alice, from sex trafficking. Instead, Boy Bishop and his followers killed Snowman but then revived his corpse using Saint Nicholas's recipe for raising the dead.

Nicholas, the Saint, inspired the cult led by Boy Bishop, an ex-society kid and heir to a fortune. He'd turned against his class, like Castro, Lenin, and others.

The Catholic Church was uneasy with this saint. While Saint Nicholas revived dead children, (*Concerning his miracles, Nicholas is reported to have resurrected over 100 dead children, including several who had drowned together: —Catholic Culture*), thousands of priests however used them for sexual gratification. Though slandered as a pedophile, Nicholas was opposed to sexual slavery; therefore, he was an outlier as the church had to cede more of its property as lawsuits piled up, launched by those who were violated by priests.

So unpopular was Nick among the Catholic hierarchy that Boy Bishop, leader of a cult of Eco terrorists called the NIKs, was forced to leave the priesthood when he showed too much enthusiasm for Nicholas.

Nicholas's gifts rivaled those of the Lord's. Not only could he revive the dead, but he was ubiquitous. He knows when you are naughty or nice.

So, by rescuing two women, Alice and Barbara, from prostitution, the NIKs were following the career of St. Nicholas, the rescuer of prostitutes.

> Saint Nicholas has been a recognized protector of women ever since he rescued three young women from a life of prostitution. When he learned they were to be sold into such a life, he secretly left gold on three different occasions to provide dowry money so they could be married. Thus, Saint Nicholas is a patron saint for victims of sexual slavery and human trafficking as part of his protection of those who are oppressed and vulnerable. — St. Nicholas Center

While Boy Bishop was away fundraising in the Hamptons, there came a clash between Brother Andrew, Boy Bishop's right-hand man, and the fake Black Rasta, a hustler who had familiarized himself with the legend of Saint Nicholas, which was required reading among the NIKs. He found that Nicholas had a partner named Peter, a Moor, who was carried to the Netherlands during the Spanish occupation. The con man took the name Black Peter but was temporarily overshadowed when the real Nicholas and Black Peter appeared from wherever legends reside. Individuals began attributing their lives' improvement to a visit from the actual Black Peter.

The fake Black Peter who had infiltrated the NIKs knew these visitations had nothing to do with him. He got spooked. Became paranoid.

Ex-President Dean Clift was not the only powerful individual who reported that Saint Nicholas had visited them. Nick also visited Supreme Court Justice Nola Payne who was responsible for the restoration of the Clift regime by breaking the tie between the Rapture judges and the remaining conservative judges. The billionaires and right wing think tanks who owned the Rapture Congress swore revenge upon Clift who had begun sounding like Huey Long, the Louisiana populist, instead of Ronald Reagan, who like Clift was also a former model.

Suddenly, the sightings of both mysteriously ceased to the relief of the fake Black Peter. He also ran afoul of Boy Bishop's confidante, Brother James, because he wanted to replace St. Nicholas with Haile Selassie and had some of the NIKs on his side. But the plot failed, and Boy Bishop (St. Nicholas became a Bishop at age 25), who had met the fake Rasta Peter on 42nd Street where he sold fake Rolex watches, expelled him from the NIKs. Their friendship came to an end.

For revenge, the Rasta man who called himself Black Peter, kidnapped the Zombie, Snowman, and presented him as Santa Claus at the annual Madison Square Garden Christmas festival. In order for him to accomplish this deed, he had to also kidnap the actor, Rex Stuart, the former star of the soap opera "Sorrows and Trials." Stuart had been fired because he attempted to unionize the television workers. He had to pay the rent. To make ends meet, Stuart accepted the role of Madison Square Garden's Santa Claus. His job was to participate in the annual Christmas festivities at the Garden. He flew with The North Pole Development Corporation from The North Pole to New York for the annual Christmas festivities at Madison Square Garden.

Disguised as a bellhop, the fake Rasta kidnapped Stuart, tied him up, and shoved him into a closet in the basement of Madison Square Garden. He substituted the Zombie Santa Claus, the body of the gangster Snowman, and, using his fantastic ventriloquistic gifts, guided an incendiary speech through the Zombie's lips. The result was a riot.

Chapter 4

Vixen had left Sam, who lived off her earnings as a bus girl and ticket taker, while he painted. That was their arrangement. Instead, he sat around smoking pot all day and by the time she got home, he'd consumed so much dope he suffered from brain fog. He'd ask you to repeat a question a number of times before answering. He had stopped bathing and giggled a lot. Craving munchies, he blew up to 300 pounds. Spent a lot of time scratching himself. Sometimes he'd insist that they draw the shades. He kept looking out of the window at cars. Said that the Deep State was following him. Vixen finally had had enough.

She applied for and got a job with North Pole Development Corporation ("Big North"), which had a monopoly on the sale of Christmas products. This required that she move from New York to North Pole, Alaska.

She landed in the communications department, writing press releases and managing Big North's web site. She'd studied Communications in college. She had an affair with a Native named Flinch, with a surname pronounced Sa.VAGE, accent on the second syllable. He worked for the Forest Service.

Flinch had graduated from Oxford, where the amount of the Indian in him had been diluted, but he still respected the customs of the Natives. This being an in-between worked for many, but his being an in-between two cultures led to a drinking problem. But then there came a crisis. Former president Dean Clift's wife, when she was the First Lady, insisted a certain spruce tree become the White House Christmas tree. She'd seen this tree during a trip to Alaska and liked it. Considered sacred, a native Big Man, an elder member of the Hawk Clan, stood in the way of those sent to cut down the tree. He chained himself to the tree. The Indians started protests in town as the men hired to retrieve the tree were waiting for Sa.VAGE to persuade the Native Big Man to move away from the tree so that they could cut it down. Tribal elders wouldn't budge. Not only did he rebuke Sa.VAGE but called him an Apple, red on the outside, white on the inside. Frustrated, Sa.VAGE's drinking problem became worse. There was an incident. In a rage, Sa.VAGE picked up Vixen's aide Blitz and threw him against the wall. Shortly afterwards Sa.VAGE met his death when he fell or was pushed into a vat of boiling Xmas chocolate. A mother made the newspapers when she found a human tooth in her child's chocolate bar

Despite the objections of the tribe, the tree was cut down and sent to the White House. When Dean Clift's wife, Elizabeth, lit the tree for Christmas, she was electrocuted. President Clift isolated himself in the living quarters of the White House. He began drinking heavily. One night he was visited by Saint Nicholas, who escorted him to the American Hell and showed him the fate of former politicians who made bad choices. Like Nelson Rockefeller whose name will always be connected to the murder of Black prisoners and their working-class white prison guards at Attica. Truman who was led by his generals to bomb Hiroshima and Nagasaki. Eisenhower, a segregationist who ordered the murder of Patrice Lumumba. Ronald Reagan,who called Black people, "monkeys." Daniel Moynihan, who accused Black women of "speciation," and likened Black people to "children," agreeing with Richard Nixon who referred to African leaders as crooks.

By now addicted to power, Chief of Staff Rev. Clement Jones leased his soul to the Devil in exchange for the Devil's assistants disrupting ex-president Dean Clift's return to Washington. And this was done. The Devil has a lease on the soul of the country's most powerful Christian nationalist leader. Rev. Clement Jones (T.2's) made a letter of Agreement with the Devil and signed the book Sir Walter Scott cites, in exchange for the Devil's interrupting former president Dean Clift's triumphant return to the capitol on a bright, sunny winter's day. The lease would be renewed annually.

Chapter 5

Burned again by her choice in men, Vixen moved back to New York and got a job with a newspaper called *The Brooklyn Nerd*. She was stirred by Santa's fiery populist speech which she saw on North Pole television before leaving Alaska. Her editor gave her permission to interview Rex Stuart, not realizing that Stuart had been kidnapped by the fake Black Peter and that the imitation Rasta Peter had substituted the Zombie form of Snowman, the hit man hired by Joe Baby to eliminate Boy Bishop who had brought Barbara and Alice off the streets. A hotel employee directed her to Stuart's room. She paid him 100 dollars to let her in. No Stuart. Instead, she found the Zombie form of Snowman the gangster, propped up in a chair. She heard the door to the room open. She hid in a closet.

The imitation Rasta came into Stuart's room. While giving the Zombie water from Tarpon Springs to keep him going, he began talking to the lifeless form which only became animated upon his instructions. He was boasting to the Zombie about how he had fixed Boy Bishop and his second-in-command, Andrew, though he was beginning to waver. He'd tried to strike a compromise. Andrew resented Boy Bishop's long absences while he held up the fort, paying bills and keeping order among members of the cult, the NIKs, a cult that was devoted to performing the works of Saint Nicholas. The NIKs cult was divided between those who sided with Boy Bishop and those loyal to the Rasta who thought that he was all that. This fake Rasta was born in New York City and grew up in the projects on Avenue D. He had a fake Jamaican accent even though he'd never visited Jamaica. Two Black members of the cult pegged him as an imposter all along. They mocked and ridiculed him. They were Barbara and Alice. But James, Andrew and the others dismissed their warnings. The cult consisted of whites whose only experience with Blacks was with their servants. But the Bishop's aides were becoming impatient with Boy Bishop and were vulnerable to the imposter's appeal. Besides these types are historically attracted to crazy Negroes.

Andrew resented the publicity that Boy Bishop was bringing to the cult. *The Times* covered his appearance at the first night of the Metropolitan Opera season. Attending galas at the Metropolitan Museum. He could be seen in the society pages having lunch with Truman Capote's Black Swans. Little did they know that Boy Bishop was plotting the murder of their husbands, who made profits from global warming.

Chapter 6

As Vixen hid, the Black imp occasionally let out an evil spine-chilling cackle. She heard him call the police. He told them that Boy Bishop and the NIKs had caused the chaos at Madison Square Garden. After the call, he almost collapsed under his giggles. As he was about to leave the room, she sighed. Hearing the sigh, the fake Black Peter started to inspect the room. He approached her hiding place. Finding nothing, he left the room. She was so shocked at what she had heard and saw that she was found wandering the streets, babbling incoherently. The phony Rasta and his dummy Santa Claus had abandoned the premises, his nefarious deed having been accomplished. The police took her to Beth Israel Hospital, where Rex Stuart, who was freed from a basement room where Black Peter had placed him, came to visit her. He gave her an exclusive interview which got her a promotion at *The Brooklyn Nerd.* Her interview with Stuart about his kidnapping made the headlines of *The Nerd.*

That was just like Rex Stuart. He was a generous person having been raised by Quaker parents. As for Flinch, her former lover, a mother made the newspapers when she found a human tooth in her child's chocolate bar.

Vixen quit *The Brooklyn Nerd* after the publisher asked her for a date while his wife was on a trip. Her father and her mother, both teachers, had established a trust fund for her. With her inheritance, Vixen traveled the country. Her politics changed. She was even part of a movement that petitioned the Hatch Rapture Congress to designate the states of Washington and Oregon as white nations. The Rapture Congress refused, fearing that those states might secede and choose Termite Control as the leader of a separate Republic. She and others then organized an armed march on Washington. It failed because the day that the armed white nationalists were to meet coincided with Superbowl Sunday. Besides, the Hatch government decided that they already had plenty of white Nationalist states. The whole center of the country and the South were red. Only Vixen and a few others showed up for the march. The others were glued to their TVs and wolfing down Buffalo Wings. Seeing that this group wasn't serious, she moved on. She heard that Termite needed a communications head. She got the job as Termite Control's communications officer, even if it meant working with his aides, whose cage names were Gut Bomb and Meso Thelioma. Like Termite Control, they were former Octagon entertainers.

Meso quit the sport when he got a flying knee in the head by an opponent and had to be carried out on a stretcher. An ex-champion, Gut Bomb, became a "cop," a fighter on decline who was used to test the talents of up and comers. The numerous concussions he received led to a deterioration of his mental faculties. He was forced to retire. Before he became a presidential candidate,

Gut Bomb, Termite Control, and Vixen. Changing his image, Termite wears a suit.

Termite ran a training camp that had to file for bankruptcy. He had a podcast that had millions of subscribers. So when he organized the movement sarcastically called D'Roaches by their enemies, millions signed up. Gut Bomb and Meso told a lot of fart jokes, and under their breaths called Vixen a cunt and other misogynist names. They resented her working for Termite.

When asked why she would work with a man whose sexual tastes were bizarre, Vixen's answer was that whatever happened in a bedroom between consenting adults was nobody's business. In a follow-up question, the reporter asked if such relationships really were consensual. She said that none of the women said no and hurried from the room. She'd abandoned anarchism and white nationalism for an extreme form of libertarianism.

Chapter 7

The real Black Peter got a letter from the authentic Nicholas, who like him had also disappeared. Nick was responsible for the conversion of Dean Clift and Nola Payne. Black Peter, the authentic one, was a sort of an equalizer who fought for the underdog and urged individuals to change their behavior. One of those on the staff of the home where the Secretariat had placed him managed to smuggle in the letter.

> Dear Peter, I finally found out where the Secretariat placed you. There's a lot of chatter around here. He ended "The Terrible Threes" with you living in some land beneath Haiti where humans communicated with animals, something he borrowed from Black folklore. This was one of his lies. He'd already made up his mind to abandon you, and that fake ending was a warning to his characters that he created them and can eliminate them. As for me, for some time, I have been an enemy of the Church, and during the Christmases of "The Terribles," I became an enemy of the State. But all of that might change with this new pope, a Black fellow. He might redeem my reputation as well as revoke the sainthood of Junipero Serra, whose soldiers raped thousands of Indian women in California. He's even talking about awarding sainthood to Sinead O'Connor and Mary Lou Williams.

His marriage to Nance Saturday's ex-wife Virginia has caused an uproar, but it will probably die down. You know, we both showed up to counter imposters who were defaming us, but after I showed Nola Payne and Dean Clift the light, the Rapture coco pops had had enough. Nola's vote broke the tie between the Rapture judges and the remaining conservatives who still had seats on the court, that declared Dean Clift's removal from office by his enemies unconstitutional. I'd also persuaded Dean Clift, who was elected because he was a hung hunk, to change his politics after I gave him a vision of American Hell. Eisenhower's status has changed, however. In "The Terrible Twos," Secretariat claimed that Eisenhower was misled by the Dulles family. No, it seems he was aware of Lumumba's murder. He ordered it.

Clift's motorcade was returning to Washington when some of the Devil's assistants showed up on motorcycles and took him to some unknown destination. They were able to trap my particles, which had been unknown to them, and place me here where other enemies of the state are held. As you know, while you were given to performing good deeds and being touchy-feely with influential folks who had fallen off the right track, I was showing personalities with power how they've been had. Even a turkey. So they told me that if I didn't leave America, they'd bring up that old scandal. You know the one. Some guy named Darryl Walker, Jr. on a podcast named "Zone of Non-being" called me a creep: "**Santa Claus Has the Habits of a Pedophile.**"

"The entire profile of Santa Claus would merit a criminal investigation if it belonged to anyone else. After all, he is a grown man who devotes all of his vigor to other people's children. Does that sound normal to you?! Go ahead: try going to a playground and handing out 'gifts' to random youth. It will take all but 2.5 seconds before their parents intervene and suspect you of being a pervert."

I just didn't want them to reveal a rumored wrongdoing to the millions of children around the world who believe in me. Peter, you know those rumors about me being a pedophile are all over X. Unlike the Catholic church which has harmed children, I'm the one who rescues children. I suspect that this is a meme that originated in the Vatican under Benedict. They're still out to eliminate me unless this Black pope makes them stop. So Peter, I'm back in the Netherlands preparing for my arrival into the city.

They can have their fat guy in the red suit. I'm outta here.

You will be missed.

Nick

Chapter 8

We have an explanation why Saint Nicholas who converted Dean Clift and Nola Payne disappeared, but why did the authentic Black Peter disappear, something that baffled the fake Black Peter, both their appearance and disappearance. As one critic noticed, Black Peter was not even mentioned in *The Terrible Fours.* Alone in his suite at the Home for Discarded Side Kicks, the real Black Peter reflected on his fate:

> Secretariat thinks he can appease me by offering me good food and drink and a 55-inch TV screen. Organic chocolate. Dutch coffee. Diet Coke. Books. A two-bedroom suite, a chef and a maid. He thinks that he can keep me off the scene by storing me here. Liar. That's this Secretariat for you. Cast you aside like you're nothing. In his "Conjugating Hindi," he made his character Chappie Puttbutt an example in case other characters get ideas. Erased him. He's like Paul Blessings in his novel "Juice!" Supported O.J. Simpson but then turned on him when the price was right. You can't trust this guy. Look at how he treats his critics. Fools them into thinking that each "Terrible" is his last, but now he wants to erase me. Like one of those political paintings in a totalitarian state, which were doctored so that enemies of the state were brushed out.

Few people to talk to here. Hardly anybody. It's a haven for the dour. The embittered. Like that kid over there, Dick Grayson. His creator had him killed over and over again until he was replaced by Stephanie Brown, a girl with hippie parents. He sits alone. Moping. Reading books about his past glory. Illustrated books. He walks around in a red tunic, yellow cape, green gloves, green boots, green spandex briefs, and a utility belt. He says that his family were members of the circus troupe who were murdered. Then there is Sam. A Black man who sits at the piano dressed in a white dinner jacket and bowtie. He plays "As Time Goes By" endlessly. And that kid sitting over there dressed like a movie Indian. Rode around with an adult. He's called "Little Beaver." You've seen him in a hundred Western movies. Red Ryder and Little Beaver. Shunned as a stereotype. Little Beaver was played by a white man, Robert Blake.

Despite the phony ending to *The Terrible Threes* where Secretariat cast me off to some mythical island underneath Haiti, one of his endless tricks, this was my actual destination. Boy did that throw off one of those reviewers, including a Black praying Indian, a Squanto hired by a witch named Rebecca. Praying Indians were like the Puritan spy, Squanto, an Indian whose highest ambition was to reach the Englishman's heaven.

It turns out that after Secretariat's book *The Terrible Threes* was published, such a continent underneath Haiti was found. While the muse of some writers is a good-looking woman, maybe playing a harp or a lyre, Secretariat's muse is a Coincidence. Only a few muses remain for male writers. Most of the muses began writing themselves.

On the first day in this place, this guy came toward me. He wanted to be friends. He called me "buckaroo." I shoved the guy. I said get away from me with that buckaroo shit. Gabby Hayes. Are you surprised that I speak that way? That's because I'm getting over my goodie-goodie ways.

In *The Terrible Threes*, I helped people. A drug-addicted Hollywood musician, a Japanese American woman whose favorite bookstore is in London, who had fallen in love with a former Manhattan literary lion. A lion at the gates, no less. I facilitated their consummation and her Anglicization. I even gave self-esteem to a turkey who was ridiculed by peacocks who thought that they were all that. So why did he place me here? There's nothing to do. Just a bunch of figures talking about their former glory. Has-beens. I hate ping pong and pinochle. Secretariat's trying to cover his ass. How did ABC's Stefan J. Boss put it on December 22, 2016:

> **Dutch Santa Claus and helper Black Pete mired in racism debate**
> By freelance contributor to Australian ABC News, Stefan J. Bos in Amsterdam.

The Black Pete character first emerged around the same time in a children's book, "Saint Nicholas and His Servant," in which Black Pete is a Moor who accompanies St. Nicholas on his annual journey from Spain.

Now, more than 150 years later, they point out Black Pete embodies negative stereotypes of black people during the colonial era, and should be banned.

The United Nations lent weight to opponents, saying it promotes "discriminatory practices and stereotypes".

Chapter 9

At one time, Secretariat was like one of those who would rush into a burning building of controversy. His mistake? He figured that if artists Betye Saar, Joe Overstreet, and Robert Colescott could take stereotypes and mold them into something opposite to what their creators intended them to be, so could he. The art world term for this kind of process is "reconceptualizing." Another term is "reimagining." Saar could turn the watermelon, used to embarrass Blacks, into a sacramental meal. In an interview, Saar defined her artistic goals as that of taking negative stereotypes and converting them into positive ones.

Overstreet painted an armed Aunt Jemima instead of the image used by Quaker Oats, which was inspired by a mammy character portrayed by a white man wearing a black face. The inspiration for Aunt Jemima was Billy Kersands' American-styled minstrelsy/vaudeville song "Old Aunt Jemima," written in 1875.

It promoted the image of the happy contented slave found in the works of pro slavery writers. For Colescott, Shirley Temple is Black and Bill Robinson, her sidekick, is white. David Hammons created a white Jesse Jackson.

The four artists took stereotypes and turned them upside down or twisted things around so that it fit into their artistic narratives. They disassociated these images from their usual associations.

Secretariat's attempt boomeranged. Whites wearing black faces caused a disturbance during the Dutch Christmas. Maybe the reason that the artists succeeded and Secretariat failed with Black Peter is that Saar, Overstreet, Hammons and Colescott dealt with ancient stereotypes, which had lost their potency, while we're reminded of Dutch whites doing blackface every December. How can watermelon be controversial? When the younger generation thinks of watermelon, they don't think of a Black farm boy sitting on a fence enjoying it while grinning as in some early ads found to be so offensive that they are now ensconced in museums. The Z'ers think of watermelon as something that you buy in Whole Foods. Organic. How many Z'ers or Milenns know about Bill Robinson and Shirley Temple? And that's what Secretariat tells himself.

It took underground cartoonist Spain Rodriguez's passing to tell Secretariat that he'd gone soft from the time in the 1960s when they were all living in downtown New York City giving the one percent the blazes. But that's when he couldn't raise the rent from month to month. When he had to sneak out of an uptown hotel because he didn't have any money. That was when he lived in a cold downtown apartment with no heat. He subsisted on Ukrainian cabbage soup, 25 cents, and a knish. Had comfort doused the flame that was once within? The younger generation calls Secretariat an anachronism. Those who would become hopping mad, were you to insult them with racist homophobic, sexist epithets, feel free to address Secretariat's generation of 70 and 80-year-olds with ageist epithets. Critics who haven't followed his strong output since the 1970s say that Secretariat "peaked" in the 1970s and thinks he's a literary Bernard Hopkins or somebody. They are up and coming writers who have positions with publishing houses, and theater producers who won't even respond to his emails.

He has a better chance of getting a play produced in China than in Harlem.

The next morning, they called Black Peter for breakfast. But he had escaped from the Sidekicks Retirement Home. The bars on his window had been ripped apart as though they were pretzels. Black Peter disappeared from the Sidekicks Retirement Home as he did in *The Terrible Fours.*

Chapter 10

Over the years, readers have claimed that, when reading Secretariat's novels, they get lost. Well, sometimes he's as lost as they are. He writes like he composes music. Composing music, he doesn't follow the chords demanded by "the standards" or "modes," which means using the scales of all of the chords included in a particular key, but he moves around like Steph Curry, the basketball player who will not be hemmed in by parameters. He refuses to be confined to the Minor/Dominant/Major 2,5,1 or 1,6,2,5 patterns of the standards. At one point, he became bored with breaking down the chords of standards, the kind of monotonous repetitions one hears on Jazz stations all day but played as though in a trance. He called it spirit music. Uncharted. Like there's a Not Through Street sign on Broadway in Oakland. He regularly turns into that street. His writing and composing are like this. Turn into cul-de-sacs. But maybe more drive throughs than dead ends.

While some writers write the outlines demanded by publishers in order to obtain a contract, Secretariat refuses. *The Terrible Fours* sold about 1,000 copies. Most writers would quit after that kind of reception. But *The*

Terribles, a forty-year-old project, have survived some of their critics. They keep on truckin' and prophesying. *The Terrible Twos* (1982) predicted the collapse of the Soviet Union and named the city where the revolt would begin, Riga, Latvia. The CIA director at the time, Robert Gates, said he hadn't a clue that this would happen. Critics asked why the popes? What is he up to? White writers have filled the library stacks with books in which popes are characters. Secretariat questioned AI about this. "The search results show numerous historical fiction, thriller, and general fiction books focused on the papacy and the Vatican." The popes in previous *Terribles* were leading up to a Black pope. *The Terrible Fours* introduced a Black Pope before Secretariat had read that Nostradamus predicted a Black Pope would appear before the Apocalypse. Another surrogate wanted to know why Secretariat used the Devil as a character in his fiction, when it goes unquestioned when white writers have written novels and plays in which the Devil appears. Such double standards make it impossible for a Black male writer to succeed in the United States, though a few get through, even though the late Elizabeth Nunez told *Poets and Writers* that American publishers only want "girlfriend books" from Black writers. When Secretariat said the same thing, Gloria Steinem got one of her kitchen help to take him down.

The Terribles are like Br'er Fox. Sets traps for critics for whom there is no briar patch for escape. Because of the greed of the fossil fuel industry, which ranks profits over survival, the planet has become increasingly uninhabitable. What could be more apocalyptic than that? Blacks are always on call to save dying Western institutions, so why not the Vatican?

He should have known that if he were to introduce Black Peter, he'd get Krampus. Also an ancient Christmas figure. Krampus's specialty is family separation. He'd kidnap children, place them in a bag and carry them across the border. The new Krampus also separates families. Only he is modern. No sacks. No climbing down chimneys. He places them in detention centers where they are exposed to sexual predators, maggot, bugs and worms in the food and overcrowded conditions. Thousands will never see their parents again. And unlike the children in the Dutch Christmas traditions, these children haven't been naughty.

Krampus

As the United States approaches the first half of the 21st century it assumes the spirit of Krampus. While food deprivation is now commonly used as a weapon of war abroad and in the United States, the U.S. is becoming sloppy and obese. Its waistline keeps expanding. Eliminating food stamps for millions. Cutting off aid to millions in Africa, India and elsewhere, a measure that will cause millions of deaths. Denying aid to the disabled, seen as surplus people. Indifferent to school children blasted to smithereens as assault weapons destroy their bodies. Guns are the leading cause of death among American children, which is all you need to know about the Krampus heart of millions of Americans. Though these policies were implemented by the Hatch government which was headed by a Christian nationalist Chief of Staff Rev. Clement Jones, Termite Control, the rival of the Hatch government, considered these measures soft and even left wing. He called the Hatch government the radical left. Krampus times. While real Black Peter represented empathy, the face of Krampus is cruelty.

Chapter 11

"It was when I went to the Quinnipiac tribal website that I discovered the legend that [Hobbomock] was really a good giant who taught the people how to care for the land and the water and how to commune with nature and grew unhappy and angry when people lost their ability to communicate with the animals."

The Legend of Hobbomock: The Sleeping Giant
by Jason J. Marchi and Jesse J. Bonelli | Nov 1, 2011

The Puritans claimed Hobbomock was the Christian Devil in disguise, but the Algonquians took a more balanced view of this deity.

This is what happens when someone discovers that they've been lied to. The conquerors have turned their gods into devils, gods invoked to resist the invaders. The word "devil" did not originate in the nations whose gods were designated as such but from the old English word "deofol." An imported word.

Gods of rebellion were thereby slandered. And so a member of the Algonquin tribe who has been Anglicized might be surprised to learn that Hobbomock, whom the invaders cast as a devil, was really one who wanted to protect the land. He resisted the English invasion and warned his people not to accept their ways.

In *The Terrible Fours*, Hobbomock returns, as Earth as a livable planet is running out of time and reaching the point of no return, and tames the Devil, who, according to historian Sir Walter Raleigh "brought America under his 'fearful servitude.'" The Devil, who like Hobbomock, and Secretariat was hard to "pin down." He posed as an antique dealer in Salem, Massachusetts, awaiting the return of his nemesis. He wanted to offer him a fourth temptation. The book *Gumbo Ya Ya* was wrong to assert that the Devil lived in New Orleans. He ventured South once and vowed never to return except for brief forays and in disguise. Don't worry. The South proves time and time again that it's full of the Devil. Sterling Brown wrote a poem about it.

While searching for Essences in the South, the Devil ran into Sam, a tall handsome Black man from whom other Blacks sought "consultations." His card described him as an herbalist. He wore a top hat. Half of his face was white and the other half was black. He was constantly smoking. The Devil decided that he and Sam, his rival, couldn't occupy the same time.

The Devil caught Sam and was carrying him to Hell when Sam asked if the Devil was thirsty. He said "Yes," and asked Sam to turn him into a dollar so that the both of them could have a drink at one of New Orleans' bars. The Devil granted his wish, only Sam stuck the Devil into his coin-purse and wouldn't let the Devil out until he agreed to grant Sam twelve months more among the living. The Devil agreed and Sam let the Devil out of his coin-purse. When the twelve months passed, there came a knocking on Sam's door. It was the Devil. He was there to take Sam to Hell. Enroute, they passed an apple tree. Sam asked whether they could get a snack on their way to Hell. While the Devil was up in the tree picking apples, Sam carved the equilateral cross at the bottom of his hooves and so the Devil couldn't come down. Sam said that he'd let the Devil down if he left him alone and allowed him to loiter about cemeteries forever. Not to say that the South is not a hell for Blacks. But if as a succession of popes have said that the Devil walks among us, who is running Hell? Do we need a woman to break the glass ceiling? Do we need a Queen of Hell and if so, who would that be?

Chapter 12

Sir Walter Scott, in his book *Letters on Demonology and Witchcraft*, reports that the Devil requires his subject's signature in his book. During his stay in Salem, he had gotten generations of Salem's men, women and their children to sign his book. He had spies in every household. Every twenty years, he'd adopt another appearance and make up stories to explain the disappearance of the former owner of the shop. His favorite explanations were that the former owner had moved to another town, was bought out, or retired.

In *The Terrible Threes*, Jones had a nightmare about a cartoon devil who appeared at the Washington bordello run by Lucy Artemis, but the devil who leased his soul was suave, multilingual, seductive. He knew all about different wines. Very few will forget the day when crowds of Washingtonians and those from parts of the country came to Washington by train, bus, plane, and car to witness Dean Clift's triumphant return to the Capitol.

Even though the weather was minus 10 degrees, crowds had lined the streets. Police on horseback were in charge of crowd control. Cardinals, White throated sparrows, Dark-eyed juncos, House Finch, Carolina

Wren were out in force. A mountain of flowers was evident in Dupont Circle and along the route where Clift's cavalcade would travel. High school bands were prepared to march in a parade. The confetti was ready. Thousands of supporters were situated behind barriers prepared to cheer the leader who defied the oligarchs who were responsible for his elevation. Dignitaries were prepared for him to join them on a viewing stand. His enemies, who were subject to mass arrests, were making preparations to leave town. In a hurry. The crowds were disappointed when it was announced that the cars had been lost. The Devil had kept his end of the bargain. His assistants had interrupted Clift's journey and kidnapped him and his men. The individual responsible for the disappearance, Rev. Clement Jones was the real power behind the Hatch administration. He amassed a fortune and owned three homes in Texas, an estate in Maryland, and a yacht he named Magdalene. He was known as the oligarch's favorite minister.

Supreme Court Justice Nola Payne's vote had rendered Clift's removal from office unconstitutional. In *The Terrible Fours*, she is killed in a traffic accident, about which there were suspicions.

In *The Terrible Twos*, during a nationwide address, President Clift read the Bill of Rights, reminding the nation of its commitment to liberty. Rev. Jones told his followers that it was a communist doctrine. But Clift blundered when he said that St. Nicholas had visited him. They removed Clift from office and hustled him into a private asylum. His loyal aides took residences near the asylum. They had faith that he'd return to power.

Rev. Jones' followers in Congress made Vice President Scab's life so miserable that he resigned rather than succeed Clift. Rev. Jones's followers used deadly tactics. They'd come into your home and assault you. Dox you. Troll you. Swat you. Threaten your children. Send anthrax through the mail and with the aid of fundamentalist billionaires, start a harassment campaign on social media and finance hackers to malign your name. They would A.I. you and make up fake speeches that would draw the mentally unstable to you. They would send a pizza delivery to your home, a signal that they knew where you and your children lived. And so Jesse Hatch was selected by a Congress in which the Rapture representatives held power. The deal was that he would appoint Rev. Jones as Chief-of-Staff. Under pressure from the Rapture followers, Clift had created the Office of Morality as a sop to the growing Rapture movement headed by Jones, so Jones was in a favorable position from which to launch a takeover. This made Rev. Clement Jones the most powerful man in Washington because he knew Rev. Hatch's secret and used this knowledge to render Hatch impotent.

Chapter 13

Dean Clift's daughter, Anne Chuck, had hired Detective Nance Saturday to find the eco-terrorists, the NIKs who murdered a short, fat, ugly oil baron. Her husband. Word was that she only married him to acquire investors interested in purchasing blue-chip works of art. She'd had a child by the oil guy; the child suffered from Down Syndrome, but the child had gifts that normal people lacked. The NIKs, an ocean worshipping cult, led by Boy Bishop the black sheep of a prominent merchant family, had taken credit for the murder, but the NIKs had gone underground and could not be found. When they sent out a communique from their headquarters, Nance Saturday, the detective whom Anne Chuck had hired, noticed a termite crawling on the wall behind where they were seated.

Using his anthropoid mode, Nance had kidnapped the Termite Queen until her bodyguards yielded the address of the NIKs' upstate country hideout. Bros. James and Matthew had been captured, but Boy Bishop was not to be found. Before that, Loathsome Larry and Police Commissioner Brown had forced a diminished fake Black Peter, now a drug dealer, to reveal the cult's

Manhattan address, but when they arrived, the cult, possibly tipped off, had deserted the townhouse. So it was Nance who found their upstate hideout, but his method had to remain a secret. As a result of Nance's tip, they traced the cult to the upstate farm and surrounded the structure until members of the cult marched out. No Boy Bishop. The police burned the farm and left, believing that Boy Bishop had been incinerated.

Chapter 14

Sir Walter Raleigh wasn't the only one who believed in the existence of the devil. He has to be believed, because in missionary school we were taught that Sir Walter Raleigh was among the smartest men who ever lived. Raleigh wasn't alone in his belief that the Devil walks among us.

On May 24, 1987, during his visit to the shrine in Foggia (in the Italian region of Apulia), John Paul II asked Saint Michael the Archangel for help to fight against the Devil, "because the Devil is still alive and at work in the world. In fact, the evil that is in it, the disorder we see in society [...] are not merely the consequences of original sin, but also the effect of the dark and infesting activity of Satan."

Who could doubt the existence of the Devil? Hadn't Pope Francis, a representative of God on Earth no less, agreed with Sir Walter Scott and John Paul II that the Devil is a living entity? In his complete works, Sir Walter Scott mentions the Devil 1248 times, and Washington Irving, 99 times, Poe, 137 times and Hawthorne, 212. Each generation of American writers must give the Devil his due. But now the Devil was disarmed, and his powers dissolved except for the ability to read minds. Hobbomock had relieved the Devil of his powers except for that talent. Now he had to earn a living like everybody else.

Hobbomock had told him to get the fuck out of America after he fumbled the transfer of Clement's Essence to him and so he had to return to Europe which, in one cartoon by Amiri Baraka, is his home.

And so, when the boss was depleted of his powers, the Devil's assistants lost their powers too. They vacated the Vatican, where they'd been installed for hundreds of years, but only now did they make their presence known because of the election of a Black Pope. They saw a Black Pope as a threat to the Vatican, one of their earthly hideouts. In opposing Cardinal Cunningham for becoming the third Black Pope, known as Miltiades II, these devils saw themselves as defending Western Civilization, but instead of thanking them, priests were sent to get rid of them.

The Vatican's buildings had been expanding and contracting, and a smell of rotten eggs pervaded the air of Rome, prompting an exodus from the city. Coming from the Holy City, odd howls could be heard. The little devils' resistance to being evicted from the Vatican had been such that priests sent to exorcize the place had failed. Some were sent to hospitals and others to asylums. If the sub-devils were defeated, one of the popes who enabled the molestation of hundreds of thousands of children could no longer rely upon their protection. He might get turned over to the Hague.

Little Devils flee the Vatican.

Chapter 15

With the demons from the Vatican gone, the Black Pope could now move from the Summer Palace where he'd been holed up until the exorcism of the Vatican was completed. He had vowed to clean house. Remove all of the sin, grime and corruption that had accumulated over the centuries. From the popes who blessed the slave trade to Pope Pious XI's drug habits and his praying for a Nazi victory over the then Soviet Union to the cover-up of pedophilia scandals by Benedict and John. But it didn't begin with them; the evil of Pope Nicholas V preceded theirs.

In 1452 and 1455, Pope Nicholas V formally supported Spain and Portugal's mass kidnapping and enslavement of Africans because it would help to Christianize enslaved people.

The papal bull (or decree) *Summis desiderantes affectibus*, issued in 1484 by Pope Innocent VIII (1484-1492), specifically addressed the malign presence of witches and witchcraft in the Holy Roman Empire and authorized a formal inquisition into their activities. The late Pope Francis, who was supposed to be modern, could still get off a slur against LGBTQ, though at the end of

2023, Pope Francis began blessing same-sex couples. Yet even so, the late Pope Francis, the liberal pope, could be caught slipping into bigotry: "Oops. He did it again. Weeks after apologizing for using an Italian word which roughly translates to 'f-ggotry,' [the late] Pope Francis reportedly used the same term again in a closed-door meeting with Roman priests on Tuesday—right in the middle of Pride Month."

Ordinarily, the little devils abandoning the Vatican would be a cause of celebration, but Pope Miltiades II had married Virginia Nance, the popular television star, so instead of a triumphant entry into Rome from the Summer Palace where the Black Madonna was worshiped in secret, because of this marriage there was a possibility of heckling and violent disturbances once Miltiades II entered Rome.

Virgina had emailed her girlfriends that "he fucks like a star." She didn't know the truth in that statement until later.

When Nance was running a gypsy limo service from New York's metropolitan area airports, constantly ducking the airport police while practicing his detective business on the side and protecting his Black neighbors from predators out to fleece them of their funds, he met Albert Cunningham, then Black cardinal of New York. He was sometimes his driver. The cardinal knew some of the most powerful people in New York. One was Anne Chuck, the widow of the billionaire oil man who Boy Bishop had slain. Her late husband's ships were constantly leaking oil into the oceans. It was upon the Cardinal's recommendation that she hired Nance to find Boy Bishop, leader of the NIKs, who believed that her billionaire husband's life was not worthy of a bird soiled by one of his tankers. Nance's finances began to improve, especially since a talent unknown to him at the time was activated.

Chapter 16

In *The Terrible Fours*, Nance learned that his "uncle" was not related to Nance. He was a scientist. So were the women who raised him who he had been told were his "aunts." You see, Nance's embryo had been injected with the DNA of a spider. Unreal? Spiders and humans have a common ancestor. He never found the identity of his birth mother, who'd participated in the experiment in exchange for five thousand dollars.

Virginia, Nance's ex-wife, had risen in the TV world. Millions of American women followed her talk show. She appeared on the covers of leading women's magazines. She even had roles in Hollywood films. He remembered one of her famous scenes. She's in a cemetery and she's pointing to a tombstone. The grave of her dead boyfriend. She says, "I told you that if you hit me one more time, I was gonna burn your motherfuckin' ass." He remembered sitting in a theater, and he and some of the other male patrons squirmed in their seats when the women stood and applauded and cheered, turning around and looking at them to see how they were taking it, as Virginia regally exited the cemetery, her head held high. Learning that Nance knew the pope, over lunch,

Virginia convinced Nance to introduce her to him. Nance had been to the Vatican when it was suggested by Cardinal Cunningham that he'd be someone to stave off their creditors. Nance was a mathematical genius, sought after by universities and the private sector. But he preferred using his talents to protect the poor and middle class. He would set up a table in one of the Harlem parks where lines of people would tell him about their problems with high-interest pay-day loans, red lining and subprime loans. (Sept 26, 1925. Elbert Frank Cox first Black person with Ph.D. in Math.)

Chapter 17

> Proverbs 26:27: "Whoever digs a pit will fall into it. If someone rolls a stone, it will roll back on them."

Hungry for ratings, the networks dignified writers from *The National Enquirer* by including them on panels with legitimate journalists. The mainstreaming of this supermarket tabloid got its hooks on the American psyche like a mosquito defecates in the blood stream of a victim, which is known as diuresis. The American reality began to mirror the coverage of *The National Enquirer*, which sold fanciful conspiracy theories to the gullible. Stories about space aliens meeting with world leaders. And that JFK wasn't killed but was in a rehabilitation home. Just as the trashy tabloids influenced alternative facts in the United States, an alternative reality was emerging. Millions began subscribing to more and more conspiracy theories. JFK returning to Dallas, a presidential election manipulated by a deceased South America dictator. Conspiracy theories? No, the classical signs of mental illness were being exhibited by millions of Americans, including "False beliefs that cannot be changed, even when presented facts (delusions)," a definition offered by the Substance Abuse and Mental Health Services Administration. Secretariat had written a book whose subtitle was "Essays on America's Nervous Breakdown." Erich Fromm suggested that nations, like individuals, can go mad in his book, *The Sane Society.* Fromm, a German Jew who fled the Nazi regime, was profoundly influenced by the mass irrationality and destructiveness he witnessed in Germany during World War I and the rise of fascism. He proposed that a society can collectively be insane, a phenomenon he analyzed extensively in his writings. Could you trace delusions held by millions to the movie star president, Ronald Reagan, who sometimes failed to distinguish between movies and reality? It was said that the president often confused "reel life" with "real life." So was American reality beginning to appear like the contents of tabloids bought at checkout counters in supermarkets? A B-rated movie? A reality that couldn't distinguish between the reel and the real? Or could it be a case of Frontal Lobe Dementia that had infected a portion of the Nation.

Chapter 18

In the United States, Christian nationalists had gotten the gumption to assert themselves. They were tired of voting for people who ridiculed them in private, calling them hicks, retards, throwbacks and basement dwellers. (In American horror movies, demons reside in the basement.) So they got one of their boys, Rev. Clement Jones, a Christian Nationalist, to run things. But his rival for control of the Nationalist Church in America, Rev. Sunshine Mooney, hadn't forgiven Jones for the shoot-out between his followers and Jones's Rapture Party followers, over whether the Messiah would return to Jerusalem or as Cotton Mather proposed, Salem, Massachusetts. The dispute, which began as a heated theological debate, ended with guns drawn. The conference was held in Texas where many men have more affection for their guns than for their family members. Since that time Mooney and Jones had made up.

The preacher Sunshine Mooney was skeptical of the Rapture Party's claim that an End Times Ascension had taken place. He dismissed the Ascension of Bob Krantz as a case of the 80-year-olds who said they witnessed the Ascension during a cabinet meeting, to their having consumed too many double bourbons and medical marijuana. Plus Ketamine had replaced cocaine as the official drug of Washington. Too many amyloid plaques in the brain. But they still couldn't explain the disappearance of Krantz.

In *The Terrible Threes* we found out why Bob Krantz insisted that nuclear weapons be used in the operation code named Two Birds. When Rev. Clement Jones rescued Krantz, the TV producer, from a car accident near Malibu, a space alien from the planet Dido had assumed Krantz's lifeless body. The elders of Dido had sent an alien to cause chaos on earth. Rev. Jones had blamed Operation Two Birds, which would explode a low yield nuclear weapon over New York. This would eliminate the surps, illegal immigrants, the homeless, and what were called parasites by the Jones/Hatch administration. It was also a way to rid the nation of a city that was a thorn in the side of family-values America. The Didonians assigned the alien who possessed the body of Bob Krantz to promote a nuclear war that would destroy the Earth, that way curbing the ability of Earthlings to extend their maniacal use of weapons into the galaxy. The intergalactic council agreed that the Earthlings should be stopped at Mars. When the Admiral's letter was found exposing the plot, Jones blamed the plot on Bob Krantz. Jones said he didn't know what was going on. Krantz, whose body was occupied by an alien, had already tipped off the Didonians that the Left Hand Path, a cabal of billionaires and a few trillionaires, had planned to invade its planet and exploit its resources. They also planned to use Dido as a space station from which excursions into other mineral-rich eco-planets could be launched. Seeing that his regime was in trouble, Jones forgave Krantz and brought him back into the administration, but instead of continuing his mission, starting a nuclear exchange between enemy nations, Krantz fell in love with Earth. His fake wife and child, aliens, had warned that he was wavering, but after he sent messages home, about such a good time he was having as an Earthling, he was summoned to Dido to explain his abandoning his mission. Christian nationalists took his disappearance as an Ascension, a warning that the Rapture prophecy was underway.

Chapter 19

On the wall of the meeting room of the reconstructed Big North, the department store, were paintings of the Brothers Herman and George Schneider (T.2's). George died of a stroke, and Herman followed him five years later. Disturbed by the WSJ's predictions that future consumers might purchase their Christmas gifts online, which would be delivered by drones, Herman died grouchy and bitter. He commanded that his tombstone bear the words "I no longer have to wipe my ass." Big North was a name change, like when Twitter became X. Elder Marse wanted to start anew after the scandal that sent Marse to prison, Oswald Zumwalt (T.2's) got probation and was required to do 100 hours of community service. He chose to assist in a literacy program in Camden, New Jersey.

Their ambitious protege, Oswald Zumwalt, with his idea of a single Santa Claus patented by Big North (T.2's) had only led to a backlash. Crowds of revelers began wearing Santa caps, an act that defied the idea of a unified Santa Claus. And his failed scheme of a North Pole Development Corporation, which would attract millions to the theme park "Christmas Land," nearly sent the Schneider Brothers into bankruptcy. A hotshot wheeler dealer and ex-Amish patriarch, Elder Marse, was called in to save the company. Before getting the job, he was the manager at an Amish chicken plant and had to pay $10,000 for violating child labor laws when a 16-year-old immigrant was sucked into a machine and died. Meanwhile, Zumwalt, Elder Marse, Jack Frost, and other personnel of Big North were indicted for producing toys that injured thousands of children. Vixen had escaped the scandal.

Because Rev. Jones had pardoned him, in exchange for a million dollars, Elder Marse was back at Big North, greedy as ever. However, no pardon was available for Zumwalt and so he had to fulfill the judge's order of committing to 100 hours of community service. He still had a job at Big North. To prevent Big North from going bankrupt, a billionaire who lived in a home that was a replica of Mount Vernon, bought the company. He's the man who asked Jones to pardon Elder Marse.

Their colleague Jack Frost wouldn't be joining them. He and a prison guard had a sideline hustle. The guard would provide Frost with drugs to sell to the prisoners. The warden was also in on the graft. Other prisoners resented the VIP treatment accorded Jack. Lobster dinners. Prostitutes brought in from the outside. A cabin located on the prison grounds where he could go and chill out. Remove his shoes. Drink beer. Watch ESPN.

He was found one morning a bloody mess as the other prisoners who were resentful of his plush treatment murdered him.

To serve his community obligations Zumwalt became the assistant to Jamal Clark, an NYPD cop who was conducting a program called Midnight Writing During the Day, modeled after Midnight basketball. Midnight Writing was an alternative for men and boys who committed minor crimes under the Manhattan Institute's policy that patrolling minor crimes would lead to solving larger ones, a hoax. Thousands of young people had criminal records because of the institute, which was founded by Bill Casey, former CIA head under Reagan. Had he not died, he would have been indicted for Iran Contra, a scheme that led to the dumping of crack cocaine into the nation's Inner Cities. Listening to the accounts of Black men about how the criminal justice system treated them had gotten to Zumwalt, and so after he spoke up, Marse and others called him squishy and a pussy.

Zumalt suggested: "I think we should take a long look before we market this kind of game." Those who didn't look upon him disdainfully smirked or winked at each other."

Marse: "It's all legit. We can make millions."

Elbows met. Fist bumps. He continued, "Termite Control has changed the whole attitude toward that privileging sensitivity to traumatized communities shit. So what the hell's come over you, Zumwalt?"

Zumwalt said: "I've been working with these men and boys in Camden, New Jersey, who get serious time for possessing a couple of joints, yet thousands of kids were injured by those toys we put on the market, and all that we got was a tap on the wrist."

What had changed Zumwalt?

Chapter 20

Orientation was taking place for Midnight Writing During the Day in the basement of one of the project buildings. On the following Monday, afternoon classes would begin. Zumwalt's late arrival drew glances from the Black and Brown men who had volunteered to teach classes. The program was funded by a small grant. The men were autodidacts, off-campus intellectuals who had read books that were absent from the school curriculum. Jamal Clark set out the goals for the program. As he talked, you could tell that he had the respect of those assembled. He stood behind a desk that some of the students picked up from the curb. Other furnishings in the basement room were collected in a similar manner. Jamal Clark was dressed in a modest manner. A sports jacket, probably bought from Men's Warehouse. A traditional white shirt. Unspectacular sneakers. Slacks with a sharp crease. He was hairless. He was a policeman.

Clark began: "In every other image of a Black and Brown, they're either holding a baseball bat, a football or a basketball. We even have midnight basketball. At least 25 percent of NFL players in the sample had chronic traumatic encephalopathy. Basketball players sometimes have career-ending injuries. Why not midnight writing during the day?" The volunteers nodded.

"Why do Black and Brown kids have to go to prison to learn to read or write? Is it because the literature available to them has nothing to do with their experience? How many of our kids become bored with school because the curriculum supports an Anglo emphasis?" Was this going to be one of these boring woke numbers, Zumwalt thought.

"Before I forget, we're joined today by Oswald Zumwalt. He'll be with us until February."

"Hi, Oswald," the assembled said in unison.

"He will be assisting me." Zumwalt had been handed copies of the reading list, which he passed out to those assembled. There was silence as those assembled began to read the list. Zumwalt raised his hand.

"Yes, Oswald."

"There are no classics on this list."

"Whose classics are you speaking of Mr. Zumwalt?"

"The canonized Western classics. "Zumwalt responded. "*Moby Dick*, *The Odyssey*, Jane Austen, William Faulkner, Shakespeare."

Clark answered, "Well, first, they get enough of that in Anglo schools, whether private or public. This is a place where they can find out about their literature. Shakespeare was more open to Black writers than you. Would that surprise you?"

"Look, you're wasting my time if you're going to throw out a lot of identity garbage."

"Check out the Black playwright, Terence."

"Never heard of him."

"Well, stick around, Mr. Zumwalt. You might learn something."

The class was finished, and the men exited. Zumwalt approached the desk, saying "Mr. Clark, I don't want to pull rank, but I've received degrees from some of the best schools in the country while you're just a cop. So every time you try to invoke that Woke shit, I'm going to challenge you."

"Well, that may be true Mr. Zumwalt, you did graduate from one of the best universities, but I'm teaching the class and if you don't do the work that you've been assigned, I'll report you to your parole officer and you'll be in Riker's Island before you know it. I expect you to manage the attendance, distribute the poetry written by the students to the class and perform whatever duties I assign you."

"It's like that, huh?

His question was answered by Jamal's smile. Zumwalt stormed out.

Chapter 21

Before going to the first midnight writing class, which would be the first session attended by students, Zumwalt decided to get a latte at the coffee shop located near the projects. After it was prepared, he looked for a table. On the wall were paintings of Black kings and queens, and Malcolm X, Sojourner Truth, Harriet Tubman. Seeing the class leader, Clark, he asked whether he could join him. The request was granted. Clark put down his book, Margaret Walker's *Jubilee*. Zumwalt glanced at the title.

"Margaret Walker? Never heard of her."

"Her novel tells you about slavery, the Civil War, and Reconstruction."

"What's wrong with *Uncle Tom's Cabin*?"

"Magnificent writing, but its view of slavery is from the outside. Walker's view is from the inside. The telling of the American story has been one-sided. Until we get the inside and the outside of the American experience, the American story will be incomplete."

"I think that's the problem with your class. You plan to bypass the classics to promote inferior literature." Clark smiled. The waitress brought Clark his breakfast. Clark began to conduct banter with her that had her smiling.

Zumwalt used their interaction to excuse himself. He took the project elevator to the basement where a room had been set aside. Present were about 35 men ranging from age 16 to 65. There was a mixture of Black, Browns, and a few whites, Zumwalt among them. Like Zumwalt, they'd been assigned to community service instead of serving time.

The chatter stopped when Clark entered, saying "Mr. Zumwalt will you call the roll?" Clark addressed the group.

Grumbling, Zumwalt called the roll. Those present answered, "Here."

Clark addressed the group. "I'm your instructor, and I'm a cop. Like thousands, I attended a community college but dropped out to join the NYPD. I've had some poetry published in some small magazines, which is why the department okayed this appointment. Let me tell you, the lack of a degree shouldn't prevent you from enjoying a rich intellectual life. One of the reasons that you have made mistakes is because you lack an understanding of where you come from. The schools didn't provide you with that information. Their idea of an education is that a superficial acquaintance with the history of a handful of European countries makes you smart. There are scores of European countries which are neglected by the Anglo curriculum. In the 1960s, Black artists like Sun Ra, Abbey Lincoln, the writers of Umbra and the Black Arts movement rejected this curriculum. They glorified Egyptian civilization, which was ruled by Black kings from time to time, but what about sub-Saharan civilizations? The five thousand years of great kingdoms. Men, and yes women rulers like the Ndlovukati of Eswatini. It was the Europeans who brought patriarchy into Africa. They did the same in India, which unlike Christianity has women gods."

Oswald Zumwalt raised his hand. "I'm a white man. What does all of this Black stuff have to do with me?"

"I will cover that. I will bring in lecturers who will cover the traditions of those members of the class who are not Black or Hispanic. Lecturers who will tell you what you were before you became white." Zumwalt sank into his seat. Puzzled. What did he mean by, "before you became white." A young Black man raised his hand. Clark acknowledged him.

"Why should we trust a cop? I got stopped a dozen times because of that Stop and Frisk shit."

"Stop and Frisk was declared unconstitutional. But you have a right to be suspicious. Many cops haven't gotten the message. Aren't screened. Thousands of cops nationwide have racist leanings. Anti-Muslim. Anti-LGBTQ+. But there are some of us who believe that the best way to reform these seemingly intractable institutions is to work from within. This is not your old NYPD. Changes are being made. Now I want all of you to tell us about yourselves."

Zumwalt listened as the men told of offenses that would have landed them in prison. He participated in a scheme that injured thousands of kids. Yet, he was receiving probation and a job at Big North, thanks to the intervention of a billionaire, who himself had gotten away with murder, killing his personal trainer. While some of these men and boys received hefty sentences for committing crimes like shoplifting, or possessing a couple of joints, Zumwalt left the class with Jamal's question lingering in his mind. His genealogy? Where did he come from? Never gave much thought about it. His father never discussed it nor did his mother. Except for an admiral named Elmo R. Zumwalt Jr., his mother's cousin. After a few drinks, his dad would brag about the Admiral.

Zumwalt did a Google search. Up came a speech by the admiral.

> IT IS EVIDENT THAT WE NEED TO MAXIMIZE OUR EFFORTS TO IMPROVE THE LOT OF OUR MINORITY NAVYMEN. I AM CONVINCED THAT THERE IS NO PLACE IN OUR NAVY FOR INSENSITIVITY. WE ARE DETERMINED THAT WE SHALL DO BETTER. MEANWHILE, WE ARE COUNTING ON YOUR SUPPORT TO HELP SEEK OUT AND ELIMINATE THOSE DEMEANING AREAS OF DISCRIMINATION THAT PLAGUE OUR MINORITY SHIPMATES. OURS MUST BE A NAVY FAMILY THAT RECOGNIZES NO ARTIFICIAL BARRIERS OF RACE, COLOR OR RELIGION. THERE IS NO BLACK NAVY, NO WHITE NAVY—JUST ONE NAVY—THE UNITED STATES NAVY.

A liberal? His Dad often sounded like George Wallace before Wallace saw the light.

During the following days, Zumwalt learned a lot about what these Black men had endured in their lives. The everyday slights. The unprovoked micro and pico aggressions. The knowledge that a Black man's murderer might not be punished or even become rich through defense funds raised on their behalf. He absorbed the poetry that appeared on the reading list at which he'd previously sneered.

Chapter 22

"We can sell millions of these games," Marse told a room full of North Pole Corp. executives. Marse who had black hair in *The Terrible Twos* was now graying. Instead of the tall broad shouldered Marse, he now walked stooped over. He addressed Zumwalt, who had objections to the toys. "Maybe you're not fit for this organization. You haven't been the same since you've been hanging out with the brothers." The executives laughed.

"You're right." Zumwalt rose. Stashed his papers into a briefcase and left the meeting room. With Zumwalt out of the way, Marse showed the salesmen and brass the new video game. Called "Snatch and Grab." Masked robbers are shown pouring out of a department store with their arms full of loot. The player gets to mow them down with an AR-15. Marse continued his pitch: "Millions of American parents will buy these games. The games will steer their adolescents from streaming porn. Millions of parents will thank us for not submitting to this gender-neutral toy shit." The demonstration was followed by cheers and applause from the gathering of executives. They all went to the hotel bar and celebrated by getting drunk.

Before returning to his apartment, Zumwalt decided to buy a pint of Vodka and sit in Central Park. It was a bright New York day. There were people sitting on benches, women and men pushing strollers, skaters. He found a bench where he could sit alone and read. He pulled out a flask and took a swig. He began reading the paperback he'd brought. A jogger ran past him and then stopped.

"Ziggie?" He looked up. There were only a few people who called him that. It was Jane. He'd lived with her, but now she seemed a stranger.

"Jane. How are you?" They'd had differences. Mostly about politics. She was wearing shorts, sneakers, and a sweatshirt. She sat down next to him. He hadn't seen her since she came out of the crowd when he surrendered to detectives for his part in Big North's scandal. She was proud that he faced the music instead of running away. "I was proud of you when you took responsibility for those foul products Big North put on the market. I didn't know that you had a conscience."

Zumwalt took another swig and offered Jane some. She accepted his offer. "Still Vodka. Boy, we used to drink gallons of this stuff when we lived together."

"I remember."

"So what are you up to?" She asked.

"I was required to do community service. So I'm working as an assistant to a workshop leader in Camden, New Jersey."

"A workshop leader of what?"

"It's called Midnight Writing During the Day. It's an alternative literacy program for people convicted of non-violent crimes."

"You, assisting in a literacy program, I don't believe it. You read few books when we were together." Zumwalt didn't say anything.

Jane looked at her watch. "I gotta go. Me and my boyfriend are having guests tonight."

"You and your boyfriend? What does he do?"

"He works on Wall Street. He's doing quite well. We just bought a six-million-dollar condo."

"And you?"

"I got a job at Bloomberg's." She kissed him on the forehead and disappeared into the crowds.

Imagine that, Zumwalt thought. *When they were together, she was in some radical group whose aim was to expose the predatory schemes of toy manufacturers. Now she and her new boyfriend had carved a niche inside the establishment, while he was doing community service and liking it.* He returned to his paperback. *Roman Comedy: Five Plays by Plautus and Terence.* How do we know Terence was Black? Unlike the prologues of other writers, he uses his to complain about his critics, a writer after Secretariat's heart. Like the Anglo woman who accused him of "settling scores." Well, we all can't be Mahatma Gandhi, whom some would call a pervert. Sleeping naked with little girls.

The prologue for Terence's play *Adelphoe* ("The Brothers") begins: "Since our playwright is well-aware that his work has drawn Unfair scrutiny and his critics are bent on passing negative judgements on the play we're about to perform. He decided to testify on behalf of himself and his work: 'You'll be the judges of whether it deserves praise or scorn.'" Way to go Terence.

Press Release

Three Arrested for Operating High-End Brothel Network

Wednesday, November 8, 2023
For Immediate Release BOSTON – Three individuals have been arrested in connection with operating sophisticated high-end brothels in greater Boston and eastern Virginia. Commercial sex buyers allegedly included elected officials, high tech and pharmaceutical executives, doctors, military officers, government contractors that possess security clearances, professors, attorneys, scientists and accountants, among others.

The acting Attorney General was happy that the Rapture government was in a state of collapse. Rapture members were always asking him to probe conspiracy theories, like how JFK Jr. and his father hadn't shown up in Dallas.

Chapter 23

It had been weeks since President Hatch had exposed the crimes of Rev. Clement Jones. Jones had run out of money. He had put on a disguise. Gone were the White House limousines. The jet at his disposal. He took the bus to the home of his friend, the Black Justice of the Supreme Court, Herman Whorst.

Justice Whorst was in the library of his mansion, sitting in a chair, wearing only his shorts and an undershirt. He was sweating and panting. He was watching one of those TV channels. You know the ones. People were moaning and crying out in ecstasy. The video excited him. His phone rang. It was one of his billionaire benefactors, Arthur Sparks. Sparks was set on rebuilding Hitler's mountain retreat at Berchtesgaden. Speaking in a whiny phony musical baritone voice on the phone, the judge said, "Yes, Mr. Sparks, me, and the wife enjoyed that trip to the islands off Greece. What a big old yacht you have. My, my. It's bigger than the one owned by the head of Acme Oil. That's the yacht on which he gave me and the Missus an all-expenses-paid trip to Mexico last summer. And thanks for sending that gift of $300,000 to the Missus. It was a wonderful, unexpected

Christmas gift. I'm glad that you sent it in a brown paper bag instead of in a form where it could be traced. These Jew progressives in Congress are trying to embarrass me. And that fucking Black caucus. Things they call me. Hurt my feelings. Now Sir, anything you want me to do for you on the court, just holler. I'm here at your disposal. Now that these Rapture nuts are on the run, we responsible conservatives will be back in control of the court. You want me to vote that way? I got it. Consider it done. Goodbye, Sir." The phone rang again.

Supreme Court Justice Whorst thought to himself, "Boy, Pierre Choderlos de Laclos was right when he said, 'revenge is best served cold.' Look at me. A South Carolina farm boy sitting on the Supreme Court. Who would have thought it? Those hi-yellow types at Yale who shunned me because I was too dark and called me 'country'—eat it cold motherfucker! Those progressive white women who tried to deny me my seat. You can forget about your freedom of choice, cuntses and cuntsettas. No matter how much marchin' and demonstration. Eat it cold motherfuckers. Those smartass guys who got higher grades and made fun of the way I talk. You can forget about your voting rights. Eat it cold motherfuckers. Those siddity bitches who wouldn't date me at Yale. Eat it cold motherfuckers."

The Justice went back to the video and was pleasuring himself when his bodyguard entered. "O, I'm sorry, Sir."

The Chief Justice displayed a constant lecherous smile like someone who'd just heard a dirty joke. "I told you to knock before you entered this library. What is it?"

"Rev. Jones is outside. He wants to see you."

"See me? He's all over the news. His very presence will put heat on me. Throw him out. Termite Control told me I can stay on as a Supreme Court Justice as long as I do what he says. Suppose he finds out that Jones entered my home."

Jones burst into the Supreme Court Justice's library of beautifully bound unread books. He wasn't his usual sharp dresser. He was disheveled, having been on the run. His poker partner wasn't glad to see him.

"Clem, what the fuck. Didn't you see that press conference? I don't want any of that shit tacked on to you to affect me. Put a contract out on your mother. Get the fuck out of here."

"You wouldn't have this job if it were not for me."

"Man, you're more toxic than Covid. I can't be seen with you. If having ordered your mother murdered was not enough you had Admiral Matthews assassinated because he was about to expose Operation Two Birds, this cockamamie plan to destroy New York and blame it on Nigeria. Now a billionaire is sending a car to meet me for lunch. And Termite wants me to stay on, maybe make me chief justice. I can't be seen with you."

"But I thought that we all agreed that building a nation based on Biblical truth required extraordinary steps?"

"Murder? You crazy motherfucker, get out of my house. Ralph," Chief Justice Worst hollered. His bodyguards, two big guys entered, picked up Clement Jones and threw him to the sidewalk. A real downfall for a man who only a few days before was the most powerful man on earth. The chief justice went back to his

Rev. Clement Jones flees Chief Justice Whorst's home.

magazine. He had to find some way to fulfill his sex drive. His wife was once young and beautiful but now she looked like a barn covered with a dress. They'd taken to sleeping in separate beds. He wanted to avoid getting crushed. The phone rang. Chief Justice Whorst picked it up. It was Gut Bomb. He told the chief justice that Termite had a list of things he wanted to get through the court. First, overturning the 19th Amendment and taking a second look at the Emancipation Proclamation. "The Emancipation—what?" But before he continued Gut Bomb had hung up. People were already calling him names like traitor and quisling. But if he went against the Emancipation Proclamation—*Holy Mackerel,* the chief justice thought, slowly bringing a handkerchief down from his forehead to his chin. *These white folks is a mess.*

Before Hatch's press conference, nobody would recognize Clement Jones on the street. Clement had collected precious diamonds, bars of gold and cash amounting to a billion dollars, but now, since the scandal, his bank accounts had been frozen, his home had been raided, and all of his bribes had been confiscated. He was now hiding in one of Washington's homeless encampments. He was hungry and needed some food. He stole a can of Chef Boyardee's Beef Ravioli from a grocery store. Nobody caught him, and he was heading back to the encampment when a man recognized him. "Where the fuck is my Ascension? I sold everything because I thought I would ascend; you fooled everybody." Some others recognized him, too. He began to run.

Clement's father was a multi-millionaire televangelist who died in the arms of a New Orleans hooker in a cheap room of a hotel that had dirty sheets, the smell of mildew, mold and dry rot and a TV with rabbit ears—you had to kick the thing to get it to operate. There was no hot water in the bathroom; the sink was smeared with what looked like blood. The walls were thin, so you could hear stuff like, "Motherfucker, now look what you made me do." Jones had no options. He called his lawyer Fred King and arranged for a surrender.

CHAPTER 24

Lawyer Fred King (T.2's) divorced his wife and moved from New York to Washington where he joined a prestigious law firm. Their 2-year-old son (T.2's) was now enrolled at Brown University. Fred arrived at the courthouse with the disgraced former Chief of Staff, Rev. Clement Jones. His surrender had been arranged beforehand. There was a herd of reporters and onlookers, among them hecklers carrying signs. Rapture devotees were praying. Those who hadn't dismissed the Rapture as a fraud. There was one man holding a sign that showed the Rev. in a prison outfit. Those opposed to the Rev. bore signs that showed Jones in the electric chair, The hecklers were overwhelmed by the Rapture followers who were singing Rapture hymns like "Lift Me O Lord from This Earthly Prison."

Sirens were heard as clashes occurred between those who came to Washington demanding their Ascendancy and those petitioning for the rights of Necrophiliacs. Smoke bombs. Molotov cocktails. Tear gas. Rubber bullets. Tasers. The only factor that diminished the size of the crowd was that others who might have been among the crowd were at Dulles and Reagan airports awaiting

Rev. Clement Jones wanted poster.

flights that would take them to Dallas where JFK would soon appear.

Michael Protzman—a longtime demolition contractor from Federal Way had summoned them there. CNN reported: "By November 2021, as Michael Protzman and his followers made headlines across the country with their bizarre gathering in Dealey Plaza waiting for the Kennedys to inexplicably appear, he was no longer living with his family, his wife was preparing to file for divorce, and his business had shut down.

"The fascination with the Kennedys emanates from a QAnon mythology offshoot. The anonymous online account with a long history of false predictions and nonsensical posts at the center of the QAnon phenomena, 'dubbe,' suddenly went silent for a period in 2018, giving way to another anonymous account that introduced the Kennedy narrative.

"The Kennedy conspiracy theory suggests, without evidence, that JFK Jr. didn't really die in a 1999 plane crash and that he is working to save America. Believers claim JFK Jr. will become president and that JFK himself may walk among us again because he is Jesus Christ.

"After Michael Protzman died, a 13-year-old girl known to her followers only as 'Tiny Teflon,' became the leader of this wing of the QAnon conspiracy cult."

Chapter 25

Termite's way of sexual fulfillment was trending. It required funeral directors to hire armed guards. Pedophilia, the number one form of sexual recreation for the American one percent and the Catholic Church, was being replaced. Inside the courthouse, Rev. Clement Jones pleaded not guilty to the charges that he ordered the assassinations of Admiral Matthews and Supreme Court Justice Nola Payne or that he put out a contract on his own mother. The judge set a million-dollar bail, which was made available to Jones from a fundraising effort launched by those who were still loyal to Jones. He was then hurried from the courthouse, pushed into a car with Fred King and members of his firm, but not before being pestered by reporters.

But on the date set for the next hearing, Rev. Clement Jones failed to show up. His lawyer, Fred King had conveyed to Jones the result of a plea bargaining proposal. Twenty-five years in a country club Federal prison and a therapy dog. Rather than accept a deal in which he would die in prison, Clement fled so the judge issued an arrest warrant. He became the subject of a manhunt, and his picture was displayed all over Washington.

Learning of his rising poll numbers, Termite does a victory dance.

Chapter 26

For Secretariat, the Apocalypse had already begun. Not the Biblical Apocalypse, but a time when Earth was no longer the swingiest destination in the solar system, the other planets being too hot or too cold. A man-made apocalypse. In Secretariat's *The Terrible Twos* (1982), he noticed that the Earth's temperatures were changing.

Now, some of those whom the Puritans called "Praying Indians," those whose highest ambition was to go to the Englishman's heaven, were paid to call out the Secretariat's "obsession," as they called it, with the papacy.

Shouldn't those who pose as God's representatives on Earth be subjected to intense scrutiny?

There was outrage when the Secretariat, reacting to the film "The Exorcist," said it wasn't an individual who needed an exorcism but the Catholic Church itself that needed an exorcism. "The Catholic Church created the devil, and the Church is full of the devil…." Secretariat was quoted in The Bergen County Record, Bergen County, New Jersey, April 22, 1974. This was ten years before the cases of child molestation by priests became a worldwide story, proving that the Catholic

Church needed an exorcism more than individuals. Check out the chronology of child abuse stories and the following cover-ups by a succession of popes. Finally, it took thirty years for the Pope's exorcist, Rev. Gabriel Amorth, a member of the Association of Exorcists, to publicly agree with Secretariat.

"Pope's Exorcist Says the Devil Is in the Vatican." By *ABC News* March 11, 2010.

"His face serious, the many lines on his face clear, Amorth confesses, 'The devil resides in the Vatican.'"

> The devil is pure spirit, invincible. He is shown with the painful blasphemies coming from the person which he possesses. He can stay hidden. He can speak different languages. He can transform himself. He may be "invincible" to the formal Christian Church, both Black and white, but in Black folklore he can be defeated and even killed.

Not only did a succession of popes believe in the existence of the Devil, but some, like Rev. Clement Jones, had entered into a pact with the Devil. Rev. Jones hadn't been the first.

> Alexander VI's sharp rise to power led many contemporaries to assume this was due to a pact with the devil. Evidence of this rumor appears in the sermons of the Ferrarese Fra Girolamo Savonarola, the thoughts of the Florentine historian Francesco Guicciardini, and the work of the Venetian historian, Marin Sanudo. Depictions of Pope Alexander VI as the Devil.

The Borgia Family by Katharine Fellows

Were the praying Indians who had been assigned to take down the Secretariat attempting to protect the Vatican from one of the worst scandals in human history? Hundreds of thousands of children abused by Catholic priests. Why won't they give Secretariat credit for predicting the scandal before it happened? Eleven years after Secretariat's comment that it was the Catholic Church that needed an exorcism, not an individual, in 1985, "Father Thomas Doyle warned of sexual abuse by clergy in a report given at the US Conference of Bishops. It was ignored." CNN Thursday, June 29, 2017 in International News.

Secretariat's dwindling number of fans found his explanation, that Krampus owns the age, did not satisfy them. But what could be more Krampus than the state of the globe which will be uninhabitable because some billionaires prefer profits over the planet's health.

Chapter 27

Secretariat was sitting at the dinner table in North Oakland wondering what he had to do to acquire more readers. He thought that if he eliminated Black Peter, a racist symbol in his *Terrible* series, he would receive more clicks for his books. If he had read John A. Williams carefully, he would have noticed that Black Peter was used by the Dutch to mock Blacks. John A. Williams had warned him:

> The goddamn Europeans with their Black Peters and Black Madonnas and blackface celebrations. Five hundred years of guilt transposed into something like vague concern for anyone with a black skin.

But Secretariat thought that he should have as much freedom as visual artists. In the meantime, he'd become a Black Peter scholar. One woman sent him a book that showed that the relationship between Saint Nicholas and Peter was one of depth and complexity. With Peter deleted, he thought he would have more checkouts from Amazon. Maybe those surrogates hired to give him bad reviews for *The Terribles* would back up.

He thought that if he eliminated Black Peter, a racist symbol, from his *Terrible* series he would also receive more Kindle clicks for his books. Secretariat had become a scholar of Black Peter's relationship with Nick. Sometimes Nick controlled Peter, other times Peter controlled Nick.

Chapter 28

So, Secretariat's sister Ruth came home exhausted. She found her husband, Kondo Tush, smiling instead of his usual greeting her with the complaint that the world was against him, which is why he couldn't find a job; he seemed pleased for once.

"What are you smiling about?" Ruth asked while pouring herself a drink.

Kondo replied, "Your brother is rich, and he ain't sharing the wealth like he ought to. He's giving the money to that white woman he's married to. A real Uncle Tom."

"Why do you say rich?"

"I was sitting here running through the latest gang-banger books that I like. Something that would amuse me until I get the next insurance settlement from jumping in front of cars, and I found that your brother made $2,040,396 on his last book."

Like their mother, grandmother, and great-grandmother, Secretariat's sister was devoted to work. His mother's favorite expression was "elbow grease." Ruth had gotten a job at one of Las Vegas casinos as a Blackjack dealer. Job description:

> A blackjack dealer manages operations at a blackjack table, typically in a casino. They shuffle the deck of cards, count chips, handle money, and follow gaming regulations. Job responsibilities are monitoring each game, ensuring players follow casino procedures, ensuring accurate payouts, and teaching new players how to play blackjack. Other duties include keeping the cards and chips organized. Essential job skills include basic math and people skills.

These tasks reflected Ruth's autobiography. She would be considered obsessive compulsive when it came to tackling tasks. She kept her cards and chips of life organized. She was the administrator of her and her husband's household. She ordered the groceries. She paid the bills and the taxes. She had enough in their bank account to pay the bills for a year, in case she became unemployed. Ruth's husband Kondo, however, made a living jumping in front of cars and collecting the insurance money, which he would gamble away. He was also litigious. He even sued a woman for sexual harassment. He'd perfected the art of bumping against cars' fenders, then falling to the sidewalk and writhing and bawling as though he were experiencing intense pain. Ruth tried to persuade him to get a real job, but he said that he didn't want to be tied down to some 9-5 shit. But Kondo was getting old. The last time, he'd missed his mark and was actually injured. He'd insisted that they move to Las Vegas so he could satisfy his gambling addiction. He was at home, scheming on how to make money without working too hard. On a table in front of him lay a quart of beer, cheese dip, and a half-full bag of Nacho chips.

His bandaged leg was propped up. There were crutches positioned next to him on the couch.

"Are you sure about Secretariat's best seller?"

"I got the figures right here."

"I'll look at it later. I want to take a ten-minute nap and then make dinner. I bought a steak."

Why would a steady, stable woman be involved with a man without goals? Ruth and Secretariat's mother were beautiful, and men used their beauty against them. All one had to do was flatter them about their beauty, and they were theirs.

When Ruth mentioned steak, Kondo started salivating like the dogs in those dog food commercials when their owners showed them some red meat. Bubbles appeared at the edges of his mouth. He thought about how clever he was. Secretariat's sister Ruth didn't know that he had a little hustle on the side that kept him in beer, Nacho chips, cheese, and cigarettes. Kondo had gotten her mother, who was suffering from dementia, to send him half of her pension and Social Security checks. He told her he was using the money to place bets to make her rich. Pleased with himself, Kondo checked the reels on Facebook. An elephant was chasing two Safari tourists. One escaped, but the other fell, and the elephant stomped him. Kondo laughed until his stomach became sore.

Tush turned the TV to a children's cartoon show. Soon, he laughed so loud that he interrupted his wife's nap. He was yucking it up and slapping his knee.

One morning, Kondo Tush paused while watching his favorite children's cartoon show and munching on Nachos with cheese. He started stroking his chin and rolling his eyes, like Kingfish in the Amos 'N' Andy Show, meaning he might have found another way to make money while not working too hard. He was thinking. He'd noticed that some right-wing candidates deflected charges of racism by stationing Black supporters behind themselves while delivering campaign speeches. Their job was waving signs of support.

Later that morning, Kondo Tush went to Termite Control's headquarters. He wheeled himself into the building. His greeting wasn't cordial. When he entered, the campaign workers stiffened. They appeared to be afraid of Tush, even though in his condition he was unable to defend himself. Termite's campaign manager, 300-pound Gut Bomb, walked up to him, menacingly, his fists balled. "What can I do for you, Bro.?"

"I have a proposition for Termite."

"Hold on." The campaign manager entered Termite's office. Termite was abiding by his morning routine and reading the obituary pages. He looked up at his campaign manager.

"Nigger outside says he has a proposition for you," Gut Bomb said in a mocking fake Black accent. Termite laughed.

"He says he wants to tell you how you can get votes from the disabled and Blacks." Termite thought for a moment.

"But wouldn't that alienate our base? They hate niggers and cripples. Besides, they can't play that guilt and DEI shit on us. The Vikings, our ancestors never enslaved a single African," Termite said. He placed the obituary page on the desk. He had circled an entry about the death of a young woman. Obeying the three-day rule, he wanted to get to her while she was fresh. He summoned his makeup man, who previously worked for a wealthy mortician. Gut Bomb and Meso Thelioma wondered why he favored this makeup person. Termite was preparing for a rally.

"I think that a lot of Black and Brown men like your macho posture. Like how you don't take any shit from your opponents. Remember that episode when you climbed down off the stage and knocked that protestor cold," Gut Bomb said. "We need all of the votes we can get. Overwhelm these fucking Christians." Termite reconsidered, and replied, "Send him in."

That night Ruth came home and Kondo wasn't there. Nor were his nachos and beer. A girlfriend called. "Girl, aren't you watching TV? Your husband is on." She laughed before hanging up. Ruth turned on the TV. Kondo Tush was in his wheel chair sitting behind Termite Control. He was holding a Black Flag spray can and waving a sign, "Black and disabled for Termite Control." When he returned home, he thought that the author's sister would be pleased. Instead, she was packing her bags.

"What's going on Ruth, why are you packing your bags?

"I'm not going to live with someone who is working for that nasty man."

"But he's paying me $2000 per rally. Already polls show that he might receive 5 percent of the Black vote."

"They must be crazy like you to associate with a sick person like him. He sleeps with dead women."

"Not after three days. He obeys that rule."

"What is that smell?"

"Formaldehyde. People who come in contact with him—"

"I've never heard of anything so creepy."

"But Ruth, we live with preservatives every day."

He tried to block her way as she, having packed her clothes, was leaving the bedroom.

"Get out of my way."

"Baby, baby, can't we talk this over."

"I also found that you've been pilfering money from my mother, you...you grifter."

"I didn't force her to give me money."

"You know that she has dementia."

"She sounds logical and coherent to me," though Kush had to tell Ruth's mother that Franklin Roosevelt was no longer president, and her deceased husband wasn't her nightly dinner companion.

But Ruth headed for the door and left the apartment. Tush wheeled himself into the living room. He turned on his children's cartoon show. That made him feel better. He called Instacart. He ordered some beer, Nachos, and a cheese dip. The phone rang.

"Hold on, Termite Control is on the line."

"TERMITE CONTROL!!!" Kondo Tush was so excited that he forgot that his leg was in a cast and tried to rise only to crash into the table and knock over the cheese dip and nacho and diet coke. He couldn't get up from the floor but was able to answer the phone.

Chapter 29

BULLETIN BULLETIN BULLETIN

WITH THE CALAMITY THAT HAS HIT THE HATCH ADMINISTRATION WHAT WAS THOUGHT IMPOSSIBLE HAS HAPPENED. LUKE LOCKETT a.k.a TERMITE CONTROL IS NOW FRONT RUNNER FOR THE PRESIDENCY

Termite was spending more time with AI moguls and ignoring the base. Gut Bomb and Meso hadn't talked to him in weeks Meso said, "He's spending all of his time with these AI and Silicon Valley faggots."

Gut Bomb said, "They're like sharks, they never sleep. That's because they're always high."

"Boss doesn't hang with us anymore. He says he's going to give these guys the run of the government if he's elected. Says he's going to demolish the White House and put up the world's largest cage and invite fighters from all over the world to fight there."

"About time. Nuthin' in that place but pictures of dead people."

"I was supposed to be Attorney General."

"He said I'd be Chief of Staff."

"He said that I could run Harvard and that my girlfriend could become Secretary of Health and Human Services. She says there is no need for vaccines. She has home remedies that will cure all ills. Both of us can get rich. I'll cut you in."

There was a stir in the main room of the campaign headquarters. There were cheers. Termite had returned from an all-night party with his AI and Tech supporters.

Chapter 30

We found out why Kondo Tush was so excited that he fell over the table and crashed to the floor. He'd gotten a call from Termite Control's right-hand man, Gut Bomb. They wanted him to open a rally in some little backwater town located in California. Though California has a reputation as a progressive state, when you enter some areas, you enter Rod Serling country. Twilight Zones with palm trees. Cheers erupted as Termite and his entourage entered the stage. Thousands held up their spray cans. That included Tush, who, sitting in his wheelchair, was rolled out. He held his "Black and Disabled for Termite" sign. He was introduced to cheers. Gut Bomb gave him the text of the speech he was to read. He was rolled up to a microphone. "Now tell them why you support Termite," Gut Bomb said. The crowd was quiet.

"Ladies and Gentlemen, I represent the Black silent majority." Some cheers could be heard. "We, like Termite, are tired. I'm tired of termites crawling across our borders. Tired of termites on the radical left." More cheers. "Tired of termites in Hollywood and San Francisco." Enthusiastic response. "Tired of termites who have taken over our universities." Loud, sustained cheers. "We're ready with our spray cans." Tush held up his spray can. More sustained cheers and whistles.

"Sometimes, Termite gets a little rough on the brothers and sisters, but we see that as tough love. After all, didn't my hero Robert E. Lee say that our people needed 'painful discipline?'" More cheers. "Now let me tell you why I'm supporting Termite." Behind him, Gut Bomb, Meso Thelioma, and Termite were greeting this part of the speech with broad smiles.

"Termite is the only figure who will get my brother-in-law to pay me some of the million dollars he has earned. He thinks that because he lives in Oakland, he's beyond reach, but nobody is out of reach." Gut Bomb rose and whispered into Kondo's ear, noticing he had departed from the teleprompter. "Where the fuck are you going with this?"

Kondo continued: "There is something wrong with this man. I hear he uses a horse's name instead of his real name. Secretariat. The Kentucky Derby horse." Booing began. "He is trying to be clever and faking mental illness so that Termite won't catch him. He hides that money in one of those tax-deferred accounts, so it won't be found. And now he's claiming that the great Mel Brooks ripped him off, whose film 'Young Frankenstein' had me laughing so. It's time for the family to intervene and—"

Kondo heard Termite tell Gut Bomb and Cyclo Spora: "Get that nigger off the stage." They rose and rolled him off the stage as people applauded. Then they took Tush to the edge of a platform outside of the backstage entrance and dumped him to the ground. He fell from

Mel Brooks of *Blazing Saddles* is to Secretariat the writer, what Penny Cheney was to Secretariat, the racehorse. Brooks got the money, Secretariat the writer got the hay.

the wheelchair, asking, "How am I going to get back to Vegas?" Gut Bomb, Gum Shield and Meso Thelioma instructed a driver to take him to a bus station.

Kondo protested, "But I came down here first class." Laughing, Gut Bomb, Meso Thelioma, and Gum Shield returned to the stage. Witnessing the incident, a man offered to buy Kondo's Termite Spray Can, which had cost $1000.00, for $500.00. After accepting the deal, Tush was lifted into the van protesting all the way and driven to Greyhound.

Chapter 31

The podcaster H. Hocks had set up a studio in a Gazebo located outside of his parents' four bedroom house. He advertised himself as a guerrilla warrior fighting against the elimination of Black, Brown, Yellow and Red stories that might cast an unfavorable light on American history. Black and Brown professors were losing their jobs which provided an opening for autodidacts like Hocks. People who were not anchored to the missionary curriculum which proposed that white men were responsible for the world's creations. There were also attempts to eradicate the story of women in history. Societies that ignore the contributions of women were in a state of decline and would eventually perish.

But Secretariat's thousand or so fans were interested in why Secretariat had gotten rid of Black Peter in *The Terrible Fours*. This provided Hocks with subscribers who were still interested in this "cult novelist." He didn't know that he was about to increase subscriptions beyond expectations. He subsisted on a disability check, was unmarried and had been diagnosed as neuro divergent. A couple of entries in *The Diagnostic Manuel of Mental Disorders* applied to him. This podcaster broadcasted from a "tiny house" located behind his mother and dad's home. His podcast equipment, mike, etc. had been bought by his parents. In a broadcast, Hocks posed the question: What happened to Black Peter? Hocks explained: "Since Black Peter was missing from Secretariat's novel, *The Terrible Fours*, Secretariat's remaining thousand or so fans are baffled. Why would Black Peter, who was a personal trainer before it went viral, be missing from *The Terrible Fours* when the figure played a prominent role in *The Terrible Twos* and *Threes*?"

"Secretariat had explained that an imposter Black Peter was replaced when the real Black Peter and Saint Nicholas showed up. Secretariat further explained that the times were more like Krampus times than Black Peter times. Krampus is Black Peter's opposite." But H. Hocks defended the absence of Black Peter, arguing: "Secretariat's idea of the period being more Krampus than Peter backed up Secretariat's theory. There were other signs. Termite Control, a necrophiliac running for president, the mass shootings, and the plagues were signs." There were other signs. Iceland was witnessing its worst volcano eruptions since 1240. There were strange occurrences:

> "On August 1, a snake fell out of the sky and latched itself onto a Beaumont area woman mowing her yard. Shortly after the snake fell, a hawk flew in and tried to rip the snake off her arm, tearing up the woman's arm in the process. Eventually, that hawk was able to fly away with the snake. While there was blood and snake venom everywhere." This from KASAT 12, ABC.

After the podcast, H. Hocks, received a note from a psychiatrist who was one of his subscribers. He said he had a tip. Something that might be of the highest national importance. He was phoning from his office located on the Upper East Side. Lyft dropped Hocks off at his office. The psychiatrist's receptionist was busy at her computer. A woman exited his consultation room. She was dressed expensively. "Dr. Buckman will see you now," the receptionist said. She escorted Hocks into the room. The doctor rose and shook his hand as the receptionist left. Dr. Buckman was short, wore a heavy mustache, and was bald in the middle of his head. He was wearing a three-piece suit. He showed H. Hocks a seat.

Sitting behind his desk, Dr. Buckman began, "I have been following your podcast, and I've decided you're the person with whom I should share this information. I am Luke Lockett's psychiatrist. His mother brought him to me. Though he pretends to be a populist, his family is well heeled. Some of his forebears were waltzing in first class when the Titanic began taking on water. But I couldn't help him." And what Dr. Buckman said next nearly made H. Hocks almost jump out of his seat. "You see, he sleeps with dead women because he believes that he is dead."

"What?" H. Hocks said.

"It's called Cotard's delusion, a rare condition in which the patient believes that he is dead. It's also called the Walking Corpse Syndrome. He exists in bliss and wants the world to join him. A man like that should be kept from the nuclear button."

The doctor spent the rest of the session citing cases involving victims of the syndrome. Hocks left the office, and while awaiting Lyft, he sent the information he'd heard from Doctor Buckman to his followers on Instagram.

The H. Hocks meme went viral. Termite Control hid from the press for a week. Finally, Vixen called a press conference. The reporters began firing questions as soon as she entered the room the campaign had set aside for the press:

"Is this Cotard's syndrome fatal?"

"Explain why Termite sleeps with the deceased."

"Doesn't having a president who believes that death is blissful a danger to humanity and especially as he is someone who has access to nuclear weapons?"

Vixen responded: "Don't believe everything you find on social media. This H. Hocks is a conspiracy theorist."

"But he has been accurate in the past."

Vixen: "Hocks and his thousand or so followers are delusional. Hocks is the one who is suffering from a sickness. If it weren't for crazies' checks, and the support of his parents, he'd be homeless. He spends all day on his podcast, promoting dangerous rumors about Termite. If Termite wins the election, such rumors will be declared illegal."

With that, she hurried from the room. But her dismissal of Hocks only aroused more interest. A lecture bureau gave him a contract. He took his message to colleges and universities. Hilton Als wrote his profile in *The New Yorker*. Gut Bomb and Meso began to have him trailed. That night Hocks was asleep in the gazebo behind his parents' house when two masked men broke in and gave him a beating. His father came out of the house with a shotgun and seeing him, the two jumped over the fence. They got away, heading from Brooklyn to Manhattan. The beating ordered by Termite didn't seem to dissuade him.

Chapter 32

Rev. Sunshine Mooney was the elder Jones's rival but got along with the son. He had even become Clement's mentor. Rev. Sunshine Mooney, the acting head of Christian Nationalism in the U.S., now that Rev. Clement Jones had disappeared, called an emergency meeting of the movement's leaders. Awaiting the arrival of their leader, they chatted.

"So the fairy looked up to me and said, 'Didn't you back a candidate who was anti-gay?'"

"And what did you tell him?"

"Yeah, that was me. But lie still faggot. Ain't nothin' wrong with a little cornhole from time to time." The two slapped hands.

"So the husband comes to me and says, 'my wife is sleeping around.'"

"And what did you do?"

"I gave her a call, and arranged for a test run of that pussy."

"How did it turn out,"

"A hot piece of ass."

"Be careful. You saw what happened to Rev. Falwell, head of Liberty University. The pool boy fucking his wife as he observed the action while masturbating."

"Let's go into the john and do a few lines before that pompous ass Mooney enters?"

As Rev. Sunshine Mooney entered, all stood. He was all out of breath when his fat ass arrived at his throne. Mooney was a short guy who wore elevator shoes. He wobbled up the steps leading to his throne. His hair was all shining and greased in a style popular in the 50s. He still parted his hair. He announced:

"Gentleman. Rev. Clement Jones, who has served us in administration after administration, is on the lam. Hatch has put the motherfucker into one nasty pickle.

"He showed up and announced himself as a quadruple non-binary plus." The churchmen laughed. "He wants to be called 'They.'" More laughter.

"He accused Clement of murdering Admiral Matthews, who was about to expose Operation Two Birds."

"What was that?" A minister asked.

"Nuke New York and blame it on Nigeria. Ignorant of Africa, they had mixed up Nigeria with Niger, where yellow cake uranium was found."

"Sounds like a good plan to me," one of the deacons interrupted. "It won't be long before every other person will be African. The population of Africans will double to 2.5 billion over the next quarter century. It's time to go Malthusian on niggers. We should cut off aid to shithole countries and invite them to commit voluntary extermination."

Rev. Mooney continued: "And with Hatch negotiating a plea bargain deal with the court, Termite Control is a shoo-in for the presidency."

"That's the good news. Kingsley Scab is thinking about running."

"I thought that he'd quit."

"He did; our people made life miserable for him."

"So what do we do?"

"We back Termite Control. Now, with Clement Jones out of the way, he can start measuring the drapes in the White House. I talked to him. He said that if he's elected, he will see that every American woman's period is monitored so that they won't get any ideas about having an abortion. These motherfucking wetbacks are reproducing like crazy. Everything West of Chicago is beginning to look like Mexico. We need more white babies." He got nods in agreement with that comment. "A fucking Necrophiliac in the White House? Rev. Sunshine Mooney. This is crazy," one of the Deacons said.

"The public doesn't mind. Termite's at 46% and climbing. Besides, 'Judge not, lest ye be judged,' Matthew 5:7. Moreover the Bible don't say nothin' about Necrophilia, so I guess it's okay. He might be the God's imperfect vessel we've been seeking.

"The motherfucker is better than this radical Marxist Scab or Scabb. He despises anything Texas. Says that we eat chili dogs, breakfast, lunch, and dinner. Calls our women trashy."

"What about Bruce Cream, the guy who shot that Black home invader?"

"He's at 2%. Rumors have it that he's bowing out. Maybe we should suggest that Termite make him vice president."
"How is that Black preacher who goes by the name of John the Conqueror doing, Rev. Mooney?"

"This Church couldn't survive without John. We were about to file for bankruptcy. The Negro can preach. We've had to install videos outside the Church to accommodate the thousands who can't get inside. His adding drummers, a mass choir, and dancers—it's quite a show. He's a damned good-looking fellow. He gets up there in his purple suit, and the ladies swoon. All I and the Misses have to do is sit behind him and count the money."

"How did he get away with that story?"

"What story?" Mooney asked.

"The one about Jesus appearing before him as a hotel clerk. What a pile of malarky." The gathering laughed until they noticed that Mooney wasn't laughing. In fact, he was glaring at the man who had made the remark.

Chapter 33

John the Conqueror's root is shaped like a serpent, recalling St. John's African referent, Damballah. John's mother is a Root worker and a follower of Arthur Flowers the HooDoo High Priest of North America who had given him that name. Blues artists also mention John the Conqueror. Mississippi John Hurt for one. Also Muddy Waters and Toronto Cannon. John had made almost a million dollars distributing an evil product. Peddling this product brought him to Detroit from Manhattan as he and his friends sought to expand their territory. Because it was raining, John decided to spend the night at a motel before contacting his business partners the next day. There was no one at the desk. Frustrated, tired, wet, and hungry, he rang the bell. The lights went out, and when they came on, he recognized the man standing behind the counter. It was Jesus. Revelations 1:14-15 was correct. He had wooly hair, and his color was not white but a "burnished bronze." He had a holy smile. He said politely, "May I help you." John dropped to his knees and started to cry. Jesus put a hand on his shoulder and then lifted him to his feet. Jesus embraced this sobbing man and vanished. John slumped into one of these ugly plastic chairs that hotels have in their lobbies. Usually red colored. In those minutes, he thought of his shame, the dirty business in which he was involved. The product, the partaking of which had left hundreds of members of the undead. He cried until he fell asleep.

Someone was shaking John. His luggage was at his feet. The actual desk clerk was standing before him.

"Anything wrong, Sir?" John stood up.

The clerk returned to his position behind the desk.

"Do you want a room?"

John was supposed to deliver the product for distribution. Instead, he took a room and slept for two days. He curled up fetus-like. During those two days, his dreams conducted a film-like review of his life. The people he'd hurt. The nasty words aimed at those who were no match for his wits. The miles of hurt feelings. The miscarriages and abortions. Unborn faces screaming at him in their infant voices. The ugly tactics that were used to get ahead. He was still carrying a bullet lodged near his spine.

On the third night, he took the bags of product and flushed them down the toilet. He knew what he had to do. The appearance of Jesus meant he'd been called to preach.

Chapter 34

When the body is in a state of rigor mortis, it's hard to separate its limbs. But to Luke Lockett, a.k.a. Termite Control, separating a beautiful corpse's legs was worth it. He had applied the Vaseline to her private parts and was about to reach an orgasm. He was trying to open her mouth for that final kiss before the crescendo of his lovemaking had subsided. Climaxed for a few minutes, he lay nude next to the corpse of the brunette. He left the body on the autopsy table while he took a shower and got dressed. He was serene. For him, fucking a live woman was pretty good. But fucking a dead one was divine. When he finished, he phoned the doctor in charge of the autopsy. The doctor entered the room. Once Termite gave him $1000, he left the room.

As Termite was leaving the hospital, he approached his limousine and got the news. With Rev. Jones on the run, the Hatch government had collapsed. Now, nothing stood between him and the White House, which presented him with a dilemma. He'd only entered the race to sell the Termite Spray cans, which had made him rich. Now, he had to come up with a philosophy. Something that would go beyond his stump speech, which crowds had heard so many times that some were beginning to fall asleep or leave the stadiums.

Vixen contacted Leon Little, the arch-conservative head of the Hamilton Society, to give Termite some intellectual heft. Some were turned off by Hocks' report about Termite's Cotard's disease. They needed a distraction by announcing a bold new program. Leon Little was a guy who couldn't go to the bathroom without billionaires or oligarchs picking up the bill. He refused because he could make more money as head of the Hamilton Society than as adviser to a President Luke Lockett, a.k.a. Termite Control.

With Clement on the run, the Secret Service had to make arrangements for Jesse Hatch's surrender. They had protected Rev. Jones over the years and grown fond of him. Now, they had to protect Hatch. A man they suspected all along was a queer. Hatch was now being regarded as a hero by the Communist/Marxist far left, for bringing down the Jones clique which ruled by blackmailing Hatch. When Hatch surrendered, large, friendly crowds greeted him at the courthouse. He was in line to receive an award as a Profile in Courage. The federal judge dismissed the charges because, as president, Hatch had immunity from prosecution. Richard Nixon said an act wasn't illegal if it were performed by the president.

Chapter 35

When the public learned of Boy Bishop's escape the message that he'd always leave at the sight of a murder appeared on billboards, in graffiti, even in sky writing: "It came between you and the planet and you lost." Brother Andrew and Brother James were freed of any responsibility for the murders of the fossil fuel CEOs. Europe was burning up as fires, with lives of their own, were devasating Greece, France, England and other countries. Glaciers were melting in the Hymalayas letting loose a deluge that killed thousands of Nepalese, and those countries that were causing climate changes sent rescuers to aide the victims of their excess and greed. Boy Bishop was condemned, but he had become a folk healer, like Luigi Mangione whose murder of Brian Thompson, CEO of United Healthcare seen to be withholding payments to those customers who buy premiums. Their wealthy supporters cheered when the two were released by a judge who played polo with their father. All of the well-wishers were invited to a reception at the Four Seasons. NIKs Sisters Alice and Barbara weren't so lucky. As Black women, they were sentenced to a year in prison, as their supporters protested outside.

That week Brother Andrew and Brother James were interviewed on a local New York television.

Interviewer: You two lived with this character for years and yet you didn't realize that he was mad?

James: We were brain washed.

Andrew: He is very charismatic. And drew us into his cult. He convinced us that the best way to save the planet was to kill the CEOs who were responsible for killing the oceans.

James: When he was challenged by this imposter named Black Peter, he began losing his grip.

Andrew: He would disappear for months. Off the grid.

James: But would send us money from his fund-raising activities on Long Island. He came back to the townhouse to warn us that a raid was about to happen. He said that he'd gotten a tip from inside police headquarters. We were shocked at his appearance. Instead of dressing in robes as we were required to dress, he was wearing jogger pants and a hoodie. Dark glasses. He was wearing a backpack and reading Ted Kaczynski, the "Unabomber." It was scary. Well, we all rushed to the upstate farm, but the police knew about the hideout. We all thought that Bishop was killed by the fire but for some reason he escaped.

Interviewer: Well, you're fortunate to have escaped the clutches of this mad man. What are your plans?

Andrew: I plan to finish law school.

Interviewer: Brother James?

Brother James: Joining my father's investment firm.

Chapter 36

Phillip Slutt was feeling good. In the projects where Secretariat grew up, he would have been called a peanut-headed motherfucker, but hey, those of us who left the projects would put it in a more civilized way. We would cite a scientific explanation for his condition. We'd consult AI which has become the oracle for writers. "Peanut head refers to a facial appearance caused by volume loss in the temples, resulting in a sunken, indented look between the forehead and cheekbones."

His colleagues were giving him hi-fives the day after he wrote a newsletter in which he took the "Black Left" to task for their "fetishization" of Egyptian civilization even though thousands of sculptures of Egyptian faces have African features, The Eshu profile. He was singing a song from a musical while taking a shower.

Phillip was a fanatic when it came to his Broadway musicals. A guest left one of the frequent dinner parties hosted by the Hamilton Institute in tears because he got an esoteric point about a musical wrong. Phillip humiliated him.

These dinner parties were sponsored by the Hamilton Institute. They were created so that second and third-generation ethnics could meet Anglos. Maybe even marry one of them.

The American Dream? Europeans who were not considered white by other Europeans can come to the United States and pass for Aryans, so hard it is apparently to find recruits. You don't even have to have blonde hair. Even Blacks and Hispanics could become Aryan leaders. They were not the only ones who received a caste promotion. Indians who are not considered Brahmins in India can come to America and go Brahmin. It was genius that the institute chose an Indian to head it. His brown face distracted from the institute's flirtation with the Eugenics movement. Didn't Phillip say the bad genes of Blacks were the cause of their violence and lack of smarts. Phillip left the shower, dressed and headed for *The Record*. When he arrived at *The New York Record*, he found all his belongings strewn on the sidewalk and passersby helping themselves to them. He almost wept when he saw someone pick up his precious "100 Hit Songs from Broadway."

He needed an explanation. He stormed into the building and got on the elevator. Usually, a passenger, one of the Neo-Con columnists, would say, "Phillip, I enjoyed your newsletter in which you defended Penny, the hero who strangled that homeless bum. You must get heat from your brothers for taking such a strong stand against political correctness, and Wokeness." Yes, Phillip had written a book about Woke as a religion but had so much difficulty justifying the analogy that the book collapsed under the weight of its fragile metaphor.

But today, his fellow elevator riders were silent. Finally, someone said, "I'll bet the new managing editor has never heard of *The Merchant of Venice*. *New chief? What on Earth could they be talking about?* Phillip thought. He entered the managing editor's office. The managing editor was packing his things. The new publisher had given him five hours to leave the building, or security would remove him from the building.

"What on Earth is going on?" He asked the fired managing editor.

"They've hired a new managing editor. The boss is following other media heads. Capitulating to Termite. The boss went down to Termite's headquarters and asked the next president for advice on making the newspaper less elitist. So Termite suggested they hire one of his people to run things. I doubt whether the new managing editor has read *The Merchant of Venice*."

Phillip thought. He was way ahead of those who had surrendered to Termite. He had expressed sympathy for a Gestapo correctional officer in a column. Maybe he could do business with the new managing editor even though he hadn't read *The Merchant of Venice* either. After all, Termite had hosted European Nazis at his headquarters. *If this was the trend—maybe I can fit in,* Phillip thought. *After all, I'm the only columnist at this newspaper who sought to humanize Termite's voters.* Slutt asked for an appointment with the new managing editor. When he left the *Record*, he found that all that remained of his belongings had been stolen by vandals.

Chapter 37

Loathsome Larry and Police Commissioner Brown were having their daily breakfast at Gotham Diner, one of New York's last greasy spoons. Mayor Larry was reading a newspaper report that the Commish handed to him.

Loathsome Larry's face was aflame. He looked like a sitting beet. He was so mad. The newspaper was shaking in his hands. As the waitress poured him coffee, he looked out of the window. There'd been a snowstorm the night before. Some of the cars on the street were spinning and making an annoying whirring sound that occurs when stuck. According to the newspaper, people had first revolted against the North Pole Development insistence upon one Santa Claus by wearing Santa caps. Now they were wearing the entire costume. Some were wearing Krampus' masks, filling the void left by Black Peter, whom Secretariat had deleted in *The Terrible Fours*, in order to improve his sales.

"Larry, we'll get the sonofabitch sooner or later. He's bound to make mistakes." It had been months since Mayor "Loathsome Larry" and his running buddy, Police Commissioner Brown, had busted members of the NIKs, whose totem was Saint Nicholas. They were

Eco terrorists who believed that the ocean was a living being. The newspaper carried a story about a Fossil Fuels billionaire found dead. Celebrations broke out in American cities as Boy Bishop's fans expressed delight about this folk hero who survived the raid on NIKs headquarters.

The New York tabloid, laying on the table of the diner where Loathsome Larry and Commissioner Brown were having breakfast, carried a photo of a man in his pajamas, bloodied and laid out on the bedroom of his 100-million-dollar yacht. Was it a mob victim? No, it was the CEO of ACME Oil. His bedroom companions, two women, were spared by the killer. Having taken a sip of coffee, Loathsome Larry set the cup down. The tabloid's coverage revealed that after they raided the eco-terrorists NIKs headquarters, named after St. Nicholas, a Poseidon figure, they burned down the headquarters. They thought that Boy Bishop would have been a casualty. Apparently not. He left his calling card. A note: "It became between you and the oceans, and you lost." Something different this time, however. He'd added a list of those who would be next. The manufacturers of pesticides, heavy metals, plastics, and harmful chemicals, all ocean pollutants. Increased security was provided for these men. Because of their bad husbandry of the waters, the ocean source of an abundant food supply for people experiencing poverty had been compromised. Once bountiful lands had become deserts. Despite warnings from scientists, global warming threatened the survival of the human species.

"This is a wily, slippery son of a bitch."

"Don't worry, he'll slip up. They all do sooner or later," Commish Brown said. Their breakfast was constantly interrupted by well-wishers. Once in a while, a critic would accost the two. All Loathsome had to do was glare at the critic, and they'd move on. The punks of New York knew that glare well. Loathsome had made his reputation as a tough cop by killing a Black jogger and being acquitted. He'd added some more notches to his reputation since that killing.

He'd won the applause of New Yorkers, the types who are supporters of Stop and Frisk. A coalition of conservatives who complained about lawlessness in New York drafted him out of retirement to run for mayor.

"Son of a bitch," Loathsome kept saying, shaking his head. He had gained some pounds since *The Terrible Fours.* His age was showing. Aches and pains unrelieved by pain killers. He'd had a hip and a knee replacement. He remembered when he was one of those young officers who joined a riot against former Mayor David Dinkins. Mayor Giuliani who'd encouraged the riot had been disbarred and was now known by a photo of shoe polish trickling down his cheek.

"The MF grew up on Park Avenue, heir to a department store fortune, yet with all of those advantages the guy becomes a terrorist and leader of the NIKs. They are killing oil and coal lobbyists. CEOs. To think this spoiled bastard comes from one of New York's most honored families. One of their ancestors went down with the *Titanic.* We rounded up his followers here. They're due to serve for a lengthy time. Two of them got probation because of connections, but the two Black women got a year to think it over. When Termite gets in, he says he'll have Bishop shot on sight. None of this judicial process shit."

"You going to vote for that guy? He fucks dead women," the Commish asked.

"Well, you got all this LBGTQ+ shit. There's no difference between what he's doing and what they're doing. People are tired of this trans-gender shit. Kids are getting their dicks cut off during recess. And guys are pretending to be gender neutral so they can share women's bathrooms and get off. Plus, a lot of people agree with me. That's why Termite is ahead in the polls."

"I'm not surprised. The fucking bar has gotten lower and lower. The country is going nuts," the Commish said.

Loathsome pushed the envelope to the Commissioner. "What about if we get in touch with the descendants and relatives of Herman Schultz? Maybe members of his family know his whereabouts?"

"They refuse to come forth. They have some of the top lawyers in the country. They sneer at our requests for interviews." The mayor dozed off for a moment. Then he said:

"The NIKs had Latino, Chinese, Black, and Native American members, yet they chose this rich white boy to be their leader.

"I asked one of them. He said that being rich, if caught, Bishop would be released on his own recognizance or get a suspended sentence. Or use his money to delay the sentencing for years. He said that if he had been one of us, we would get some hard time."

"We scoured the place before we set it afire. He must have gotten tipped off that we were going to raid and escaped," the Commish said.

"Yeah, well we burned down their headquarters thinking that he died in the fire. But he tricked us."

After two more cups of coffee, Loathsome seemed to achieve a less dour mood. He began to laugh, and Brown asked him what was funny.

"I was thinking about the old days when things were simple. When Son of Sam said, 'a dog told him what to do.'" Brown laughed so loud that he attracted the attention of his fellow diners.

Chapter 38

August 26, 2026. Because of "changes in climate," a glacier snapped in the Himalayas loosing a flood that killed thousands.

Although Phillip Slutt had lost his job at *The New York Record*, he still had his job at Alexander Hamilton University. But when he reached his office on campus, he found the locks had been changed. He was furious. He went to the Dean's office. The Dean was on the phone. He was talking to one of Termite's assistants.

He signaled for Phillip to take a seat. The Dean was finishing the call: "Yes, tell Termite, his terms are acceptable. You have my word that the curriculum your people sent as a guide to study at our university is acceptable, I agree that only nice things should be said about America. How we tamed the wilderness and conquered the West. And the Woke faculty members they suggest firing will be fired at once. Yes...yes... yes, Sir. And when your aide comes to sign our agreement, we'd like to throw a grand luncheon for him in the faculty club. You said his name is Gut Bomb? Interesting name. Look forward to meeting him. And tell Termite that I have ordered my bear skin apparel and helmet." Rising he said "Phillip, delighted to see you, what's on your mind?"

Universities, journalists, law firms prostrate themselves before Termite Control.

"Why am I locked out of my office?"

"Your job has been terminated, Phillip, sorry."

"But you were pleased with me when I criticized the students who demonstrated outside of your office. My class about Victimization as an Impediment to Black Success is full each semester."

"That's the problem, Phillip. Termite Control has gotten to those who provide the school with millions in endowments. Such 'woke' courses have to be eliminated. Termite has decided that they lack an intellectual foundation." Slutt stood up.

"But I'm against Woke. Didn't you read my book, *The Opposite of Woke is not Asleep*."

"Sorry, Phillip. Now if you will excuse me." Slutt left the Dean's office.

Chapter 39

JQ said that she'd work for Nance. Not as a secretary but as a partner. Nance took this as a sign that she'd grown and he hadn't. Did that mean she would no longer get involved with bad guys like the death squad leader who was assassinated while she and he were making love? Earlier that day, JQ had entered the office and saw a spider scuttling across the floor. She fainted because the spider was the size of a mouse. Nance was still recovering from the news that his embryo was mixed with the DNA of a spider, and the spider part had been activated. Did the Russians know? Had the Russian woman whom he dated (T.2's) been a spy? Had she found out what he didn't know? Was that the reason for her abrupt return to Moscow?

The man who posed as his "uncle" and the woman who posed as his "aunt" were government scientists who were part of a project whose mission was to weaponize insects. His spider knowledge helped him find the location of the NIKs' hideout, which he did by holding the queen of the termites hostage.

He had a new office with views of the Hudson and East Rivers. But now, something had gone wrong. When

JQ recovered, he was kneeling, comforting her. His Arthropod phase had temporarily ceased.

"There was a spider, as huge as a child, crawling."

"You're okay now. Listen, I have some business to attend to. Go to Yelp and take some bids on exterminators. How are preparations for the party going?" They were having a party to celebrate the opening of their office, JQ and Nance, Inc. Nance said:

"The caterer will arrive an hour beforehand, as will the band and the bartender. We have a great RSVP list. Some of those guests are descendants of those whose ancestors had first-class passages on the *Titanic*." Nance excused himself. He took the elevator to the first floor and headed for his Harlem apartment. He wanted to get home before another episode.

Nance's "uncle" had told him that there were pills that would expel the spider part. But he'd refused to take them. Having the senses of a spider gave him an advantage over the other detectives. In his Arthropod mode, he hid in the corner of Termite's office. That way, he could hear Termite and his entourage discuss some of their plans. Extermination of undesirable groups. Concentration camps in Texas and elsewhere. Though Termite and his followers worshipped Odin, one of them quoted Samuel 15: "Now go, attack the Amalekites and totally destroy all that belongs to them. Do not spare them; put to death men and women, children and infants, cattle and sheep, camels and donkeys." This was how they viewed their Rapture enemies.

While a guest at the Vatican, Nance's Arthropod mode enabled him to listen to Cardinal Adrien, Miltiades

II's enemy, discuss the Black Pope's assassination. But now, instead of remaining at a tiny size, he was growing during the spider episodes—a big problem.

Chapter 40

Rex Stuart (T.2's) had made a pile as the star of the soap opera "Sorrows and Trials," Catering to the streaming market, he set up his film company. Right now, Afro-Futurism is hot. He asked his agents to name a Black writer who could write a series for his company. Secretariat's name came up. Someone said he'd read his novel, *Yellow Back Radio Broke-Down* (1969), and it ended with A.I. running things. Before the end of that day, Secretariat received a call from Rex Stuart. He said that he had a proposition for Secretariat. It could be a rewarding trip for him to come to Los Angeles.

Secretariat picked up his ticket at United. A limousine was waiting for him at LAX. He checked in at the Beverly Hills Hotel. This would be his third stay at the hotel. He remembered that his rooms had fireplaces. Stuart met him in the restaurant. He wasn't the matinee idol who thrilled millions for portraying the polo-playing playboy of "Sorrows." Jowly now. A paunch. Otherwise, he'd aged gracefully. Something was different about him. He had a beard. Secretariat spotted him and joined him at his table. He had a copy of *Yellow Back* that he wanted the Secretariat to sign.

“Interesting work. I can see why the critics call you, Sun Ra, and George Clinton Afro-Futurism’s fathers. In your 1969 novel Artificial Intelligence is running things, leading to the elimination of 9-5 drudgery.

You had that in your novel that was published in 1969.”

Yes, Secretariat thought, *that was before my idealism went sour.*

“Well, it’s upon us.” He said.

“This Afro-Futurist stuff is trending. What do you think of it?”

Secretariat saw it as another academic scam—an excuse for professors to lure students into empty classrooms by offering something sounding like Science Fiction. A generation that grew up on Star Trek. They could write long papers with the usual sleight-of-hand obscure writing. Some students would use AI to write their papers. Discussions about how AI would influence academia would provide Professors with an opportunity to attend conferences, sample good food, sightsee, and make dates.

“It’s popular, but the Afro-Futurists are missing an opportunity.” Secretariat said.

“How is that?”

“They could use the popularity of space travel films and art to introduce Black and Brown kids to sciences like Astrophysics. After a Black Astrophysicist lectured, he was surrounded by Black and Brown kids. They hadn’t been taught that such a field was open to them.”

“Something to think about. I don’t know whether you have seen—” Stuart mentioned a spate of films that carried the Afro-Futurist label. "We'd like you to try your hand at writing one for us." Stuart mentioned an amount of money that would pay his family's bills for a couple of years. All Secretariat had to do was write a treatment. Others would develop the story; he could withdraw his name from the production if he didn't like the result. Their drinks arrived, followed by a gorgeous meal. The next morning, he returned to Oakland.

Secretariat had binged on so many series on Netflix, Apple, Hulu, Amazon, and other streaming services that he could anticipate what a character would say before they said it and even predict the action and ending. That's why members of the segregated screenwriters' union were afraid of being replaced by AI. AI was on to their racket, writing scripts where you could predict the conclusion and the killer after viewing the first scene. They worked the old captivity narrative to death. Sixty percent of these series were about a missing white girl.

Secretariat knocked out a few pages overnight. He got an idea for his Afro-Futurist treatment on the plane returning to Oakland and developed it while taking a bath the next day. The hero of his Afro-Futurist treatment would be a musician, a trumpet player.

Chapter 41

When Dave Brubeck and Paul Desmond performed on an album called "Jazz Goes to College," they probably didn't know how prophetic a title that would be. Jazz music, whose early patrons were members of the criminal underworld, was now part of the curriculum of some of the most handsomely endowed schools in Japan, Europe, and the United States.

In Secretariat's treatment, the character with the most lines was Lester Tatum, a professor at a prestigious Northeastern college and an accomplished trumpet player. Legend has it that when Tatum performed at a late-night Jam session in Harlem, some of those Jazz greats whose names would be recognized throughout the world had praised him effusively. He was eighteen at the time. His horn was an encyclopedia. He could do Dizzy Gillespie, Louis Armstrong, Miles Davis, Clifford Brown, Roy Eldridge, Freddie Hubbard, Lee Morgan, Fats Navarro, Terence Blanchard, Donald Byrd, Bobby Bradford, Clark Terry. He knew Jazz history. He could do King Oliver and Bunk Johnson.

He could have followed the route taken by those musicians who preceded him. Years of disrespect from club owners and record producers. He could have become one of those sad casualties, those whose careers were owned by the mob and who spent their earnings buying the mob's products. Instead, after his retirement from college teaching, he spent his years teaching music in high schools, concerned that the younger generation would abandon Jazz for music that depended upon machines. He composed and produced an album when he felt he was ready instead of signing a multi-album contract, a sure route to burn out.

He loved New England, especially in the fall when the leaves turned yellow, gold, and red. The one thing about the East that Californians envied.

The Treatment:

Scene 1: When Lester Tatum arrives at his office, he finds a strange message on his computer. It is from an African location. He is invited to be a featured performer at a Jazz festival in Kampala, Uganda. His roundtrip ticket could be picked up at the Turkish Airlines ticket counter. The honorarium would be $25,000.00.

Scene 2: After Turkish Airlines lands, Tatum's hosts take him to the Sheraton Kampala. That night, some masked men enter his room. They blindfold him and dump him in the trunk of the car. When the car stops, the men open the trunk. He has fallen asleep.

Scene 3: Tatum is finally escorted to a modern club. People cheer as he enters. "Jukebox," a dancer, greets him. The clubgoers are fans and have begun to recite elements in Tatum's biography, such as significant dates, engagements, and career highlights. They tell Tatum of their plight.

A brain-eating amoeba, Alyab Owongo, which lives at the bottom of a nearby lake, has enchanted the land. Instead of resisting, the people line up at the shore of the lake awaiting their turn to be escorted below to Alyab Owongo's palace and have their brains eaten. Sometimes, these lines are a mile long. The only thing that can destroy Alyab Owongo and his rule is the playing of the lost scale. A scale that had disappeared thousands of years before. This is because a Griot was among those whose heads were fed to the Alyab Owongo, and before he died, the Griot cursed Alyab Owongo, that he would be destroyed by music. The Griot's prediction: "A lost scale will bring him to the surface."

The resistors have tried every scale available. None has worked. They want Tatum to reconstruct the lost scale.

Scene 5: Daymer, a spy for the Brain-Eating Alyab Owongo, has infiltrated the resistors. He stands before the Brain-Eating Alyab Owongo, seated on a throne in his palace at the bottom of the lake.

Although Alyab Owongo wears a uniform covered with medals, he has never fought a war. The two talk in gibberish, but we get English subtitles. Daymer informs Alyab Owomgo that Tatum has arrived and is seeking the lost scale and that upon hearing it, Alyab Owongo and his kingdom will fall. Owongo becomes so mad that he sends his militia, the Headhunters, to capture the resistance and the foreigner they hired to find the scale. The underground club is raided, but the patrons and Tatum have disappeared. They've retreated into the forest. They plan a strategy.

General Alyab Owongo.

Chapter 42

Scene 6: Africa never ceases to amaze. Tatum and his hosts find an adequate 3-star restaurant even in this forest. The cuisine includes a number of items delightful to the palette. Porcupine and crocodile meat. They are on the fourth course. The waitress engages Tatum in a conversation. She is studying anthropology at a university in Kampala. Yes, she has heard about the legend of the lost scale and that a man who claims to be 125 years old is living in the forest says that he has memorized the scale. But nobody has investigated his claim because of fear of reprisals from Alyab Owongo.

The waitress says that this would be of great interest to her and that she would guide Tatum to the place where the 125-year-old man is rumored to live. Tatum tells his party that he and the woman must set out alone. That way, they wouldn't startle the man. They find him. He is speaking an ancient form of Luganda. The woman translates. She tells Tatum that "For him to give you the scale, he wants you to accomplish some tasks." Tatum had taken a folklore course in college.

He remembers tales where the seeker is required to capture a snake, a ferocious animal, or a biting insect.

And so when she hands him a list of the old man's requests, Tatum is apprehensive. Instead of the tests one finds in folklore, the old man wants a state-of-the-art smartphone. An IPAD. A 50-inch Samsung TV. A subscription to *Business Insider.* With his American Express card, Tatum orders the items, and a few minutes later, a drone appears, and the items are parachuted into the forest from the drone.

The man and his wife, who is fifty years younger than him, dance arm-in-arm in a circle, and separately; the old man does some brilliant shuffling in his barefoot. He goes into a trance, and Tatum notates the secret scale while the old man is singing it.

That night, Tatum stands before the lake. Tatum plays the scale on his trumpet. There is a rumbling in the lake that wakes up the town. Alyab Owongo's palace surfaces, and Alyab Owongo's men, the Headhunters, swim to the shore where they are killed. Then, a thousand or so skulls float to the surface. But Alyab Owongo is missing. He escapes. He will have to find some more noses to take him in so that he can continue to suck the brains out of people. He will have to find another place to begin a contagion.

Chapter 43

Using binoculars, Boy Bishop was staring at his target. His enemies were in pursuit, but he had enormous assets because of the trust fund the department store moguls had established for him. Rich people are beyond the law. Rarely are they punished. He had come to Europe under a fake name and had rented a suite in a 6-star hotel. He chuckled as he read an account of Mayor Loathsome Larry's attempt to explain his escape from being captured along with the other NIKs. Mayor Larry thought that he'd been consumed by the fire set by the police after the rest of the NIKs were brought out of their hideout in handcuffs. He'd gotten away because he had a protector inside the police department. Anne Chuck didn't trust the police.

Charles, an enforcer, was hired by Anne Chuck to assist in finding her father. His powers diminished, the Devil was ordered by Hobbomock to send Anne the map indicating where his assistants placed her Dad and his cabinet before sending the Devil packing for Europe. Nance and Charles were supposed to meet that weekend to travel to the location where the ex-Devil had stored Dean Clift and his entourage. But first, Nance was supposed to show up for the opening of Nance and JQ's Detective Agency. JQ had left dozens of messages for him, but Nance was in no condition to answer them. With the money that he'd received for capturing the Termite queen, which led to her army giving up the address of the NIKs, the Eco Terrorists who murdered her husband, Nance had bought a brownstone in Harlem. But he could not leave the house.

His uncle had told him, when he revealed to him that he was born as a result of a government experiment, there would be side effects. He found there were advantages in being an excuse me Spider Man.

JQ was frantically calling Nance's uncle. The balloons were up. The hors d'oeuvres were being served. People were at the bar. The band was playing a medley of Ellington hits in the background. She finally got a hold of Nance's uncle, who soon knocked on the door of Nance's apartment. His uncle put pressure on the door until it opened. He fell back at the sight. The house was a mess. He turned on the lights. There was Nance. A spider as large as a man. His uncle cornered him and injected him in the head with a fluid, and momentarily, Nance was a man again, lying nude on the floor.

"What happened?" he asked, coming to.

His uncle held some pills in his hand.

"What are those?"

"The pills that will end your crisis. I offered them to you before, but you refused. You have to take one per week, or else that part of your nature will sneak up on you again. The pills contain some hallucinogens, so you might have bizarre, surrealistic dreams."

As a spider, Nance was useful in solving cases, but obviously, the harmful side effects might now outweigh the benefits. Nance swallowed the pills.

"Hey, what time is it? I've got to get to the office. Our open house is underway."

"I'll drive you," his uncle offered.

Nance arrived at the party and was greeted by well-wishers. JQ greeted him with a frown, however, but he was cheered when he saw that the place was packed. The oil baron's widow and ex-president Dean Clift's daughter had referred many of her society buddies to do business with the firm. But Nance still maintained an office in his Harlem brownstone.

Chapter 44

Phillip Slutt had run out of his severance pay from Hamilton University. He would be broke in a few months. He went to a coffee shop near Columbia where he mulled over his situation. After being seated, he looked across the room. Sitting at one of the tables was Vixen. He'd met her at a party at the estate of one of the right's billionaire sponsors. They had similar views. He walked over to her table.

"Phillip, how are you, please have a seat." Vixen was reading *The New York Record*. She placed it on the table.

"Haven't seen your column in a while, Phillip?"

"They terminated my column. I took a buyout. I haven't been able to find a position since then, and I'm running out of buyout money."

"Have you heard of Termite Control?"

"Who hasn't."

"What do you think of him?"

"I haven't made up my mind, but anybody is preferable to Hatch and Clement Jones returning to power. I was going to endorse the father of the white rapper Ice Cream, Bruce Cream. I'm all in favor of 'Stand your ground.'"

"I'm the communications director of his campaign." Vixen handed Phillip her card. "Come by the campaign headquarters. I'll introduce you to him." Nance examined the card. Vixen picked up the tab for his coffee and pastry and left the shop.

Desperate for a job, Phillip Slutt called Vixen to tell her he'd like to meet with Termite. Vixen had been trying to set up a meeting only to be blocked by Gut Bomb and Meso Thelioma. She finally reached him and made an appointment. Though Phillip was a delicate thing, weighing only about 130 lbs., Gut Bomb and Meso Thelioma frisked him as though he was a terrorist. They smirked as they allowed Vixen to pass. Termite dismissed his aides, Gut Bomb and Meso, who were trying to hang around. See what was going to be discussed.

"What's on your mind, dearie?" Termite asked Vixen, resting his feet on his desk and his head on his hands. "And who is this guy?" She didn't receive the kind of sexual advances from Termite as she'd received from Gut Bomb and the others. She wasn't his type.

"I'm your communications director, Termite, but there has been little for me to do." Vixen's face was beginning to expand, and her ankles swollen and none of her diet solutions worked.

"We haven't needed you. I'm a shoo-in for the presidency."

"You haven't heard the news?"

"What news?" Termite replied.

"Jesse Hatch has announced his candidacy for president, now that a federal grand jury has cleared him of wrongdoing while being blackmailed by Rev. Clement

Jones. He calls himself 'the new Hatch.' Since his announcement this morning, he's raised twenty-five million dollars. Calls you a disgusting creep whose sexual habits might spread disease to the general population."

"How should we respond?" Termite asked.

"That's where Phillip comes in. He was a professor at Alexander Hamilton University."

"Professor?" Termite said with a sneer. He despised academics and had vowed to take the universities and colleges under his control if he were elected. Emphasize Nordic Studies. Make white Americans revere their Viking past, though many of his followers were Mediterranean types or were from Spain, considered a backward nation to Northern Europeans, even worse than the Eastern Europeans.

Phillip responded, "Termite, you need a new spiel. Like a fresh program. "Go on," Termite said.

"People are very enthusiastic, but then you go into the same old tired pitch you've used for years. You need to put more meat and potatoes on your appeal. You need a big idea."

Termite leaned forward. "So what do you suggest I do?"

"Follow the proposal made by Alexander Hamilton at the Constitutional Convention. June 18, 1787."

"What was that?"

"He wanted Americans to be ruled by an elected monarch. When that monarch dies, another monarch is elected."

"Kinda like a King, huh?" Termite said.

"Exactly," Phillip explained, "forty-eight percent of Americans want someone to guide them. Tell them what to read. How to have sex. When to bear children. When to go take a shit."

Turning to Vixen, Termite said, "I like this guy." Vixen beamed.

"Keep talking," Termite said.

"You will have absolute power. What we're talking about is Article II of the U.S. Constitution, which vests all executive power solely in the president. It's called the Unitary Executive which means like you're royalty."

"But what about those Rapture guys on the Supreme Court? They might still be loyal to Hatch."

"As a king, you can get rid of them. Install Herman Whorst. He'll do anything you want in exchange for gifts. He likes trips on yachts. He even had a custom-made yacht cap designed with the logo Supreme Court Justice. Both he and I are detested by Blacks because we believe that white supremacy doesn't exist. Ignoring the beginning of Phillip's self-pitying speech Termite said. "Vixen, I want you to be my campaign manager and you, along with Phillip, will be my chief advisor. Now get the hell out of here and go to work." The two left the room, and Termite returned to the obituary pages.

Chapter 45

So how did Hobbomock disarm the Devil, something that Christians over the centuries had failed to do?

The Devil was on the way to D.C. to renew the contract with Rev. Jones, stopping off in New York on the way from Salem where he had posed as an antique dealer. But first he traveled to the next town where he kept his car in storage. Canned Heat was right. The Devil's favorite car is a Coup De Ville. He changed into some expensive clothes and partied his way to New York. Instead of meeting women in the woods like the old days where they would freeze their asses off, he'd rented a series of houses through Airbnb and partied with them there. Hobbomock knew that New York was the Devil's favorite town. The Devil even appeared in an ad: "When in New York, I stay at the Chelsea Hotel." And so Hobbomock set a trap for him as one would for game.

Hobbomock, disguised as a hot trick resembling Rock Hudson, lured the Devil, called a "seducer" by various popes, into a New York hotel by promising him incredible pleasure. But Hobbomock out-seduced the seducer. Made him into his little bitch, which reminds one of Junior Wells' song: "Somebody Done HooDooed the HooDoo Man." Hobbomock tricked the Devil into drinking the Devil's elixir, as the Devil thought it was gin, the Devil's favorite drink. Hobbomock gave the Devil a taste of his own medicine. The Devil, after drinking the elixir, became a little red devil, but then transformed into a middle-aged man, which is how Hobbomock left him. When the big Devil, the boss, was rendered impotent by Hobbomock, his assistants lost their powers at the Vatican where they were preventing the Black pope's entrance. The Devil's other assistants deserted the place where they were guarding Clift and his entourage.

During the White House meeting where Jones was supposed to renew the Devil's lease on his Essence and the Devil informed Jones that Hobbomock now owned his Essence, Jones laughed in Hobbomock's face because the agreement had expired the day before. Hobbomock was angry. He told the Devil, "If you'd paid attention instead of partying your way to New York, you would have noticed that the lease expired. That's why you always lose, because of your excessive hedonism. You know nothing about moderation." The Devil knew that there was truth in what he said. He lowered his head in shame.

Hobbomock rendered his punishment. I order you to return to Europe. No longer will America be under your fearful servitude. They'll have to choose someone else. Maybe break the glass ceiling. Choose a woman as queen of hell. You're done here pal." That night, the Devil, disgraced, left for Europe, which according to Amiri Baraka is the Devil's home. With that Hobbomock became a snake and slithered from the Oval Office into the Washington streets until he could find a park where he could curl up and vent. Legend has it that Hobbomock likes swamps, and his favorite disguise is that of a snake. Washington D.C. was built on a swamp because the enslavers were suspicious of permanently relocating the capital from New York City to Philadelphia, as both cities were viewed as hotbeds of anti-slavery activity. D.C. still has the smell of a miasma.

A group of schoolgirls came upon Hobbomock, and, shrieking, ran as fast as they could. He then changed again. He would return to New England. Back to the drawing board. Come up with a new plan. But before that, he'd settle scores with Jones. As a Quinnipiac, Hobbomock was proud. He didn't cotton insults.

Hobbomock was going to demand that all of those populations that were not indigenous to North America go back to where they came from. The whites had to leave within a year. Blacks, since they were involuntary immigrants, could take a while longer. That way the land could return North America to its pristine beauty before the invaders spoiled it with industrialism.

CHAPTER 46

Gut Bomb and Meso Thelioma had to read in the newspapers that Vixen and Professor Phillip Slutt had taken over the running of Termite's campaign.

"The boss is going soft. Got us wearing these faggoty assed suits, after telling people during that interview that we'd never give up bear skin and he even wears a red tie," Gut Bomb said. "Taking advice from a nigger after all of the shit we had to go through because of Kondo Tush."

"It's that Vixen bitch. She brought in this guy to write his speeches," Meso said.

"Termite told me this morning that his next speech will be the turning point in the campaign. He's getting flustered. He thought that he had it in the bag. But now Jesse Hatch has decided to stay in the race," Gut Bomb said.

"He's being interviewed. Told his followers to tune in," Meso said.

"What do you think he's up to?"

"Damned if I know. We're out of the loop."

Gut Bomb and Meso Thelioma were upset. Since his poll numbers rose, their old Octagon buddy Termite Control was hanging out with billionaires and neglecting them. Led by E. Koh Lye, a ketamine addict, they used terms like Techno Feudalism and Crypto Feudalismo when describing their goals. Termite Control, Gut Bomb and Meso Thelioma never questioned Termite's odd sexual inclinations, figuring that was his business. But now, he was lost to them. The night before, E. Koh Lyle had sent a limo for Termite. They were always whisking him off to some unknown destination. Gut Bomb and Meso were beginning to grumble. Then they read the morning paper and really got mad. He had spent the evening in an underwater apartment belonging to an eccentric trillionaire, a friend of E. Koh Lyle, who'd made his fortune from crypto currency, curency that didn't have gold to back it up.

Gut and Meso were discussing how their old Cage buddy had abandoned them for the gang of billionaires. And now this lesbian Vixen was taking over his job as campaign manager. "He'd rather hang out with queers and fish than associate with us. He used to knock out guys with a foot," Gut Bomb said.

"He's gone soft, you wouldn't know that the guy won three championships in the Octagon," said Meso.

"Yeah, well what about me? I'm supposed to get the Department of Education. Close down Harvard and the Smithsonian."

There was a commotion coming from the main room of the campaign. Termite had entered the headquarters and had fainted. When he was revived, Gut and Meso were staring down at him.

"What happened?" Termite asked.

"You went out with E. Koh Lyle to some floating island for a party."

"I don't remember a damned thing," Termite said weakly.

Phillip Slutt said, "We were worried about you."

Gut Bomb gave Slutt a contemptuous look and then looked at his watch. "Termite, the rally begins in two hours. If you don't show up, there will be rumors."

"I need to take a shower," Termite said.

Gut Bomb and Meso Thelioma were waiting for their leader to emerge from the campaign bathroom where he was taking a shower. When he finished, Termite began coughing and sneezing, exhibiting flu-like symptoms. He had a temperature of 103.

Gut Bomb had his towels ready, and a manicurist was preparing him for a nail trimming. Soon, Termite was on the way to a triumphant rally at Madison Square Garden, escorted by black SUVs, without whose manufacture, air pollution could have been reduced by thirty percent. Along the way, crowds cheered his entourage and held up their thousand-dollar spray cans. Termite had to make one more stop. 462 First Street. Gut Bomb and Meso stood guard in front of the city morgue. Termite constantly refreshed himself by having some recreational sex before a rally. The encounter calmed his nerves and lowered his temperature. He had been profusely sweating. He emerged from the morgue, and the three got into the lead car of their entourage and headed toward the Garden.

The line before Madison Square Garden was long. The faithful had turned out to hear their leader. Some of them saw him as King Cyrus the Great. Soon, Termite Control was in the middle of his usual speech before his thousands of followers, all waving Termite Spray cans. There was a plane flying above streaming Termite's favorite line, "I Am Your Exterminator."

Termite termed Muslims, LBGTQ+, and minorities "termites" and promised to send them to the Termite hotel, where they would check in but won't check out. The crowd roared its approval mixed with laughter.

"Has Congress solved this problem?" Termite asked. A resounding "no" came from the audience. "Has the Supreme Court?" Boos at the mention of the Supreme Court. "What we need is a King. Like Alexander Hamilton proposed. I humbly accept that assignment." The cheers continued for two minutes, some shouting,"Termite Control, a king forever." Termite raised his clenched fist. "No more dithering, no more lengthy reports, no more elections, no more arguing and feuding, no more conventions—" He didn't finish because he'd slumped to the floor. There was panic. Screams.

Gut Bomb and Meso Thelioma carried Termite off stage, beating back his devoted followers and putting him in a van. The van sped toward the nearest hospital. Termite was declared comatose. Doctors said that the cause of his illness was *Naegleria fowleri.* His lawyers argued that the Constitution doesn't require that a president be conscious and since his cabinet members are former cage fighters, backed by a million armed D'Roaches.

None is about to invoke the 25th Amendment, which is how President Dean Clift was gotten rid of. Plus, Termite promised to recruit a million or so of his followers as his private army.

Despite the suffering that results from those whom they send to the Oval Office, Termite's followers vote for these types on their promise that they will protect them from those whom Termite Control dismisses as lower than bugs. Immigrants from shithole countries, Blacks, Browns, and Yellows, but not white immigrants from the Nordic countries and South Africa. A newsman, asked a question of Jesse Hatch.

"President Hatch, there's a rumor that Rev. Jones leased his soul to the Devil and when the Devil came to collect, the Devil and a mysterious figure were told by Jones that the lease had expired. Jones thought it was funny. Considering the fact that Rev. Jones might be sent to jail, who is laughing now?" Hatch refused to answer the question. They left the room.

Chapter 47

Though his name would still be on the ballots, Termite's bid for the presidency was finished. Americans would never vote for a comatose necrophiliac—or would they?

But there was no reasoning with the Termites. They were anti-science and anti-logic. The fact that Termite's followers insisted that a comatose man could become president was even too much for Vixen. She packed her bags and left Manhattan for Brooklyn, where she disappeared into the café writing culture. Phillip stayed on.

Chapter 48

Upon hearing of Termite's illness, former vice president Scab or Scabb, a descendant of the Scabs who arrived on the Mayflower, had called an urgent meeting of the Sons of New England. The mood was celebratory. They'd finished their clam chowder and were now nursing their brandy. At this gathering, the group revealed that, unlike a Robert Lowell poem, they had a sense of humor. They were downright jolly at the prospect that one of their own, Kingsley Scab, who could trace his lineage to Plymouth Rock, might gain office again, which had been stained by immigrants. Dutch, Irish, and Germans—thank God no Italians or Jews. Yet. For them, the last real authentic Anglo president was their man John Quincy Adams, not imitation Anglos like the Bushes and the Lodges. Scab was greeted with a standing ovation as he approached the podium.

"Gentlemen, the latest most vile and disgusting candidate for higher office, Termite Control, is in a coma." Applause.

"A pattern of presidential decline that began with the defeat of John Quincy Adams by Andrew Jackson, a vulgar slave owner, trafficker, bigamist, Indian fighter, cockfighter who couldn't spell his way out of a paragraph yet received an honorary degree from Harvard. This so outraged John Quincy Adams that Adams said, 'I could not be present to see my Darling Harvard disgrace herself by conferring a Doctor's degree upon a barbarian and savage who could scarcely spell his name.'" More applause.

"He married his whore Rachel who was still married to her husband, yet his trashy followers called Adams a pimp, based on the rumor that he offered an American woman to the Czar for his sexual pleasure, a baseless lie." The gathering laughed and clinked their teacups. Some said, "here, here," the way they saw the English say it in Parliament.

"Jackson, a repugnant Scots-Irish hothead, was always challenging people to duels. With the fall of this cannibal Termite Control, a Jackson imitator, the true founders of our country, the descendants of Cotton Mather and his father, Increase, can once again rule and continue the policies of our John Quincy Adams." Every tuxedo rose to his feet and gave Kingsley Scab a vigorous ovation. They began writing checks, contributions to his campaign.

"Now, the next item on the agenda is the club application of a Jew." There was silence.

Chapter 49

Anne Chuck provided Nance with one of her bodyguards, Charles, to locate the whereabouts of Dean Clift and his party. She was one of the many children the handsome president sired by beautiful women. He called them "The Poon Tang Brigade," which he'd scribbled on a dinner napkin that someone found and sold to Sotheby's for $50,000, but no matter how many women came to him as though on a conveyor belt, Clift always returned to her mother, Elizabeth.

Anne was his only legal daughter. How many children he had among his 500 sex partners was unknown. She'd been in and out of mental institutions, but after a fancy Park Avenue doctor had treated her with Psilocybin, she was able to lead a stable life.

Did Nance believe that Clift disappeared because of demonic powers? Sir Walter Raleigh and Sir Walter Scott would have said so.

Charles and Nance rented a van. Nance read the directions on the map that the Devil had sent to locate the oil man's widow and Dean Clift's daughter, Anne Chuck. They found themselves in the Maryland woods. They got out of the SUV and took two shovels out of the trunk.

They walked to where the Devil said Clift and his party were supposed to be located. They spent hours following the ex-Devil's instructions to Anne. Nothing doing. They were about to give up when they heard some knocking. The sounds were coming from the van. They went to the source of the knocking and found that the son of Anne and her husband—the kid with Down syndrome—had stowed away in the van. They lifted him out. When on the ground, he tugged at Charles pants leg and pointed to a place about 100 feet from the van. He led them to a plot of earth. They could tell that the ground was different from the surrounding terrain.

As they approached the site, they heard some sounds beneath their feet. They began to dig until they came upon a door. They opened the door and found steps. They descended to a ground floor, where they found Clift's entourage. The men were sprawled on the floor of a cave. They were so thin they resembled cadavers. One whom he recognized was Clift's Secretary of State. He was seated. Leaning against a wall. There was a terrible smell. A rat scurried across Charles' shoes. "What the fuck....," a startled Charles said.

These men who were used to the finest Washington restaurants, where they were given special treatment by Maître d's, were glad to dine on the triple-decker hamburgers that Charles was thoughtful enough to bring.

After the apple pie dessert, they began to speak weakly of their ordeal. A couple couldn't continue because of violent coughing, so deprived they had been of fresh air. They told of how the Clift entourage was about to enter the capitol in triumph when the Devil's assistants riding on motorcycles blocked their way. Removed them from the cars and imprisoned them in this underground space. Charles asked why Clift wasn't among them. He and Nance were told that Clift and an aide had escaped on Halloween, the night that the minor devils raided the nearby towns to spread terror, their idea of fun.They wore ski masks. Then one day, the day that Hobbomock had disarmed the Big Devil, the little ones in the cave disappeared while simultaneously others fled the Vatican.

Charles and Nance helped the survivors into the van and began making their way toward Washington. Anne Chuck's kid was sitting next to Charles, who was driving. Having had some food and drink, members of the Clift cabinet began singing the Yale Whiffenpoof Song. Charles told them to shut up after the line, "We are little Black sheep who have gone astray." They passed an ice cream shop in one of the small towns. The kid nudged Charles. Charles stopped. He went into the ice cream shop and bought the kid a mega cone, with toppings. Nance phoned Anne to tell her that her father had not been found, that Dean Clift and two of his aides had escaped. Their whereabouts were not known. Anne was disappointed to hear this news but was happy that her father was still alive.

Chapter 50

Kingsley Scab or Scabb was working on his inaugural address, full of pomposity and false grandeur, when his wife called him into the living room. "I thought you said you had the thing wrapped up." Put a bonnet on this woman's head and she'd look like Whistler's mother.

"I do have it wrapped up, dear, with the dropout of Mr. Rice and the condition of Termite Control, I have a clear path to the Oval Office."

Pointing to the headlines, she put her finger on the line showing the latest polls. Since news had reached the electorate that Termite Control was in a comatose condition, his poll numbers had increased by ten percent. There was speculation that he might be sworn in while unconscious and his legal experts were working on how this could be done. Scab's wife reacted: "Kingsley, you're so inept that a dying necrophiliac's poll numbers are higher than yours. What a fucking loser. I knew that I should have married Harry. He's made a fortune selling yachts to some of the richest people in the world. Instead, I'm stuck with you."

Kingsley Scab wasn't listening. He rose. He was dizzy. He began to tremble and experience shortness of breath.

He braced himself by holding on to the arms of a chair. His wife headed toward the bathroom to fetch his pills. He turned blue but after taking his pills, he sat down and relaxed. She was thinking about getting a refund on her inaugural outfit.

Chapter 51

When Kondo Tush reached Las Vegas, he got some bad news. The bus line had lost his bag, which held all his clothes. When he got to the apartment, he found an eviction notice. He forgot. His wife, Ruth, paid the rent. She'd moved in with her girlfriend Gladys, a blackjack dealer. He went to the casino, thinking maybe to borrow a few bucks, but Ruth wasn't dealing. Her girlfriend Gladys was. She was sitting on a stool dealing cards to some casino customers. "Gladys, where is Ruth?"

"She has the weekend off and is traveling to Bermuda with her new boyfriend." The three customers, who were white tourists, were interested in their conversation.

Kondo asked, "When is your break? We can talk."

Gladys kept playing cards. "We can talk here."

"When will she return?"

"She doesn't want anything to do with you. She says you tried to con her brother as you did her mother. The million-dollar number that you said was money was actually the book's Amazon rankings. Your brother-in-law Secretariat's book, *The Terrible Fours*, came in behind 2,040,395 other books. The rankings number doesn't represent money, you idiot. And then you swindled her mother." Gladys kept dealing. "I'm on the job. Get out of my face." The white customers laughed. Kondo rolled out of the casino and returned to the bus station, where he found a corner and slept, sitting in his wheelchair.

Tush had spent the last of the money that he received from selling the Termite Spray can for $500 instead of its $1000 listed price. He tried to take up residency in the Las Vegas bus station again but was banned. What was he going to do? He got that look. The scheming look. With his last money, Kondo bought a sponge and a bucket from a hardware store. His leg had healed and he was capable of walking but thought that the wheelchair would help him in his new scam. So he found a little island in the middle of Las Vegas. He held a sign. "Veteran." He would roll up and down next to cars when traffic stopped and look pitiful as he asked for donations. He still blamed his brother-in-law Secretariat for not sharing his riches gained from book sales in spite of what Gladys had told him. By noon, he'd collected fifty dollars from the deception. A Mercedes pulled up. He recognized Ruth and a man who must have been the new boyfriend that Gladys mentioned. The Morehouse graduate. He was an accountant at the casino where Ruth worked. Kondo looked ahead while Ruth threw five singles at him, accompanied by a scornful laugh. He dropped from his wheelchair and picked up the bills as the Mercedes drove away. One blew out into oncoming traffic. He rushed out to pick up the dollar just as a car was bearing down on him.

Chapter 52

Crowds gathered to greet Dean Clift, after hearing that the place where he and his entourage were held had been found. They expected his triumphant return to Washington. People began gathering on the streets but dispersed after hearing that Dean Clift was missing. That he had escaped from captivity and his whereabouts were unknown.

The night before, millions tuned in as Hatch was honored as a Profile in Courage. With encouragement from the audience, Hatch was coming to the end of his speech. "Yes, I was a victim. For years, I allowed Rev. Clement Jones to make me his slave as he blackmailed me about my sexual persuasion. I was triggered so much that I was beginning to resemble Roy Rogers' horse." Hearing this reference, some of the Z Gens in the audience gave each other quizzical looks before returning to their phones. "If you or someone you know is being bullied, call this number." He held up a sign. Printed on it was a website and a phone #. "They, like me, will find agency, empowerment; they can also text—"

But before he could continue, a ragged Rev. Jones rushed on stage and shot Jesse Hatch in the stomach. As the crowd screamed and headed for the exits, security guards tackled Jones and held him to the ground.

Chapter 53

Two Nuns are in the kitchen of the summer palace having coffee. One says:

"We've been serving popes for decades but have never witnessed the goings on surrounding this pope. Ever since they were married, they haven't left the bedroom. Except for his papal duties. He and that television star that he married. These old guys in the Vatican are furious. They're talking about excommunicating him. Especially Cardinal Adrien from Spain."

The second Nun answered: "But they're scared they'll offend Africa and South America. They love this pope. The young people are awaiting his arrival in the Vatican now that those demons mysteriously left. They've come from all over the world. It's only the older people who are upset. People in their 60s, 70s and 80s. The young are wearing their hair like his. His wife Virginia changed his style. The young people are calling him "the Hip Hop Pope."

"Those little devils abandoning the Vatican meant that the coast was clear for him and Virginia to return to the Vatican from the summer Palace. People say that ugly odor that hung over Rome during their occupation has evaporated."

"We only saw the two of them at breakfast, lunch and dinner and from time to time when they'd walk around the gardens, hand in hand like love birds."

"You remember their wedding night. They were moaning and screaming so." The two laughed.

"Well at least they're not hiding anything, like the previous popes. Sneaking in young men and women at night."

"I agree, but was it necessary for them to be married by a Buddhist priest?"

"His wife suggested that. She also insisted that all of the images of Jesus as a Caucasian be sent to the Louvre. She's commissioning artists to depict him as he appears in the Bible, with wooly hair and burnished skin."

"Well, there's one thing he did that I like."

"What's that?"

"Allowing us to choose our own wardrobe. How do you like this Gucci dress? It was from a Christmas sale."

"I want one. I'll order it too."

Virginia and Miltiades II had about two hours to themselves before heading with their entourage for Rome. Before that, about twelve people entered the room. They had been assigned to dress the couple. The pair could tell that some of them resented them. With pins in her mouth, one of those kneeling to stitch together a seam of Virginia's dress penetrated the cloth and pricked her skin. There was a trickle of blood. Looking up, the offender apologized, but the apology was accompanied by an impish smile. The offender said *ho sistemato quella stronza* (I took care of that bitch). Some of the other women who were dressing Virginia

Virginia and Pope Miltiades II prepare to depart for Rome.

and Miltiades II smothered their giggles. Were they resentful because Virginia had married the pope or was it because both she and the pope were Black? Since Blacks occupied Italy for hundreds of years it seems that Italians would have gotten used to them.

After their dressers left, Virginia expressed her anger. "I started to slap that woman who pricked me," Virginia said with a hand on her hip as she lit a cigarette and walked around the room, Betty Davis like. "How can you stand it?"

"Maybe I'm on a mission to save mankind, or maybe I'm the Antichrist as some of my critics are saying. Getting into exchanges with mortals might be beneath me." They both laughed. Miltiades II was getting homesick, but what were the odds of his returning home? He would likely spend the rest of his life in Rome. It all depended upon orders from higher ups. Way higher.

"The Vatican hierarchy is upset because you made them give up their super Hummers," Virginia said, putting on her aquamarine earrings made in Brazil. "Now they're driving Fiats because of your orders," Virginia said with a smile. She went to her husband and put her arms around his neck. He felt the warmth of her abdomen against his.

"They have to get around like Jesus did. The Fiat is the modern equivalent of the mule." They laughed.

He was standing in front of the mirror and combing his hair.

"What kind of reception do you think you'll receive when we step out on the balcony?"

"They'll probably boo. Throw things."

"How can you be so calm about it?"

"They'll get used to the new situation."

"But darling, they're already upset about you liquidating some of the Vatican properties and setting up institutions that will funnel that money to the poor." Before Miltiades could respond, there was a knock on the door. It was time to make the trip to Rome.

Chapter 54

Now that the Devil had returned to Europe where the slave trade began, he had to find another way of collecting souls. Another way of stealing the Essences of mankind. Back home in Europe, he found one. The Devil had changed his name and his appearance. That's because somebody had told him that he resembled Rupert Murdoch. He'd bought a five-story townhouse in Amsterdam because he still wanted to be close to sin. He had about a dozen women working for him. Bringing money to him by practicing "the world's oldest profession." But it wasn't enough to satisfy his expensive tastes. He put up a good front, however.

The maids were cleaning up from a lavish dinner party the Devil had hosted the night before, attended by some of the Amsterdam artistic and cultural elite. The party was held to celebrate the Christmas season, even though the Devil found it awkward to celebrate the birth of his arch enemy. One of the reasons he threw the party was to read the minds of Amsterdam's movers and shakers. Get tips for making money. The Devil was used to being rich.

There were courses upon courses of the best, most expensive and fashionable foods and the finest of wines.

Though Hobbomock had deleted his powers, except for his ability to read minds, necessary for the ability to gauge marketing trends, as many Blues musicians can tell you, the Devil liked to eat good: boeuf bourguignon and bouillabaisse, tomahawk steak, turbot fillet, lobster rolls, caviar and truffles, whole roast suckling pigs, foie gras, Dover sole, and seafood towers.

At one point during the party, the Devil sang a "standard" accompanied by one of Amsterdam's leading jazz pianists. The bassist and drummer had reputations throughout Europe and were hits at the North Sea Jazz Festival. He chose the tune, "Tussen de Duivel en de Diepblauwe Zee." He impressed the gathering with his knowledge of Dutch. He had a baritone voice like Al Hibbler, but he swung the song like Eddie Jefferson and even included some scat. Then he did Jackie and Roy Cain's version of "I'm Forever Blowing Bubbles," the Bop classic, and when he got to that line "Be-Ah-Batootable-Bubbles," the motherfucker brought down the house. But the celebrants didn't notice the tear that appeared in one eye because this song was the Devil's autobiography, especially that line about trying "so hard to reach the sky." He knew that he would never be welcomed back. One legend has it that the Devil was expelled from Heaven because God was jealous of his singing ability or that he conducted the heavenly choir. He was in charge of music. Was Lucifer "The Angel of Music?" Ezekiel 28:13?

It was the afternoon of November 16th. The Devil went to the window. On the canal below, there was a procession. Boats carrying St. Nicholas, followed by ones holding senoritas. They would dock their boats on the Island of Texel. There they would be met by Black Peter. Then Black Peter would climb into a sports car and begin distributing presents; Nicholas would follow, mounted on a white horse. But the question was: where was Black Peter, and would Black Peter turn up?

There was a knock at the door. The Devil went to answer. He opened the door. Standing before him was Sam. He was wearing a black top hat and tails. His face was still painted half white and half black. He held a bottle of gin in his hand, the Devil's favorite drink.

"Sam," the Devil said. "This Injun ran me out of America, and now here you come, just as I've gotten myself a rep in this town."

"Aren't you going to invite me in for a drink? I brought your favorite drink, Gin," Sam said.

"I'm on the wagon with Gin." The Devil remembered how Hobbomock tricked him by slipping the Elixir into his drink.

How about some Rosé?" Once inside, Sam turned to the Devil. "I have a business proposition that might interest you."

The Devil didn't trust Sam after the changes he put him through, but now that he had lost his powers, he had to find some way to get by and acquire Essences.

"I'm listening."

Chapter 55

Secretariat was sitting on his porch interacting with the birds. Doves, crows, and scrub jays, who'd lined up on the telephone wires, as was their custom midday after Secretariat had finished his walk, which took him from his house in Oakland to Market Street then to 54th Street and down Genoa, reminding one that Italian fishermen once occupied the neighborhood, and then back home. These Italians who once lived in West Oakland had moved to North Oakland and prospered in the 1940s. They brewed wine in their basements. He settled into a chair and began communicating with the birds. Every October, a bird that did a 3-note Blues chord would visit.

Hobbomock would be proud of him. His connection with birds. But each morning, he'd become depressed after reading the morning newspapers. Yes, he still preferred hard copy over digitalized news. As he read, he would become so ashamed of the damage that members of his gender were inflicting on the world that he wanted to return to bed and throw the covers over his head. One dunce wanted to revive nuclear testing and was threatening his enemies with bombs one hundred times more powerful than those that exploded at Hiroshima and Nagasaki. The problem with dictatorships is that they're anti science and so the few scientists who know better are afraid to tell a dictator that were he to attack a nearby country with H-bombs, the radioactive debris would drift into his country causing millions of deaths, just as the fallout of the 1945 Trinity Tests held in New Mexico dispersed globally. Two fucking idiots were currently engaged in a competition that was leading to the starvation of millions.

Chapter 56

Try as he might, though he has a reputation as a universalist, Secretariat couldn't rid himself of his inner cultural nationalist. It's like an elf-sized nudge, like the one in that commercial where a pixie-sized Black guy is goading Charles Barkley to eat more food. Secretariat's elf is wearing an outdated dashiki, sandals, shades and is standing on his shoulder. He wears a button which reads "Black Power." He is whispering into the Secretariat's ear. He says, "You saw that Halle Berry movie 'Moonfall (2022)' last night. Why is it always the white man who saves the planet? Ponder that?" In his wildest dreams he could not have imagined that he would meet the challenge.

A shimmering spectral shape settled into the chair next to him. At 88, Secretariat was unfazed—he'd survived cancer, diabetes, and the slander and smears that come with a profession that deals with the public and where one is exposed to their opinions, good and bad. But he was doing okay in a field that was boiling over with talent, not just among the elite but ordinary people.

He had read a Harvard University study about aliens living among us. The research paper mentioned that the "unidentified anomalous phenomena (UAP)," more commonly referred to as UFOs and extraterrestrial beings, could be living underground on the moon or even walking among humans. The research also explored the idea that UFOs or unidentified aerial phenomena (UAP) could be spaceships visiting Earth-based "alien friends. Crypto terrestrials."

"What can I do for you?" Secretariat asked the spectral shape as though nothing extraordinary had happened.

"I was sent from the planet Dido. In my earthly appearance my name was Bob Krantz."

"Yes, I know you. Your career origin was confusing. My bad. It's my fault that it's unclear that you inhabited Krantz's body after the accident near Malibu, when the real Krantz was killed or did you inhabit his body before? It's hard to determine where Krantz the producer ends and Krantz in his alien shape begins. And after you were blamed for Operation Two Birds and robot Sam Beowulf was ordered to capture you, why didn't you use your advanced knowledge or call down one of your flying saucers to deal with the monster?"

"Then I would have drawn attention to myself. My mission was to blend in with the population and infiltrate the Hatch government. If I had used my powers, I would have blown my cover. "

"You hid in Nance Saturday's apartment."

"Yes, that's how I found out about his spider DNA before he had knowledge of his heritage."

"So, I should also be blamed for the lack of a transition between Krantz, referring here to your human disguise, being out favor with Rev. Clement Jones and then regaining his confidence so that you're attending a cabinet meeting when the Didonians recalled you, which the Earthlings mistook for a Rapture event?"

"Should you be blamed for something the copy editor missed?"

"Yes. It's my fault. So what can I do for you?"

"I got recalled for showing too much affection for Earth. They gave me one more chance to save Earth."

"What?"

"Didonians have the technology to destroy the Earth in 30 minutes. The Earth is viewed as a menace. The original plan was to stop the Earthlings at Mars. But extremists among our people want to destroy it now. After they recalled me, the moderates planted an alien in a high office on Earth, thinking that he could civilize the Earth savages."

"How are things on your planet?"

"It's like California without the earthquakes. Having been around for a billion years, they've eliminated earthquakes. But I'll cut to the chase. I need your advice."

"Why me?"

"We've read your books, *The Terribles*. You obviously have the gift of prophecy. We feel that you would be the person who would solve your humanity's flaws."

"I'm flattered, but I have questions."

The spectral shape was covered with intricate red, yellow, white, and black stripes like some butterflies. "In *The Terrible Threes*, you, the alien, using Krantz as a cover, were visited by two Didonians—one Black and one white." The Didonian told Secretariat that "Those two were imposters. They were arrested and sent to re-coloring camps when they returned to Dido."

"Well there is one theory that me and my fellow humans can't help ourselves," Secretariat said. "Neuroscientist Robert Sapolsky says: 'Our genetic and epigenetic makeup, together with environmental and cultural factors, make us who we are and determine how we behave, a function of the architecture of the prefrontal cortex and the neurotransmitters and hormones circulating in our body, all of which are physical manifestations of a person's genetic inheritance and the environment in which they spent their formative years.'"

The Didonian specter responded: "I disagree with a cold-blooded deterministic view of human destiny, but suppose Robert Sapolsky is right. You wouldn't want to eliminate human beings if they can't help themselves, and even if a nuclear war did occur, it wouldn't mean the end of the species. Seventy thousand years ago, Earthlings were down to three thousand people, but somehow, they bounced back. They always seem to recover, no matter the challenge."

"No, we decided against the nuclear war idea which was supposed to begin with Operation Two Birds."

"We replaced the Didonian occupying the body of Krantz with a healer. He occupies one of the highest offices on your planet." Maybe he can cure your species of its mean streak.

"Call him home."

"But why?"

"There's an expression; 'Physician heal thyself.' Give our species another 500 years. We'll be fine. We're going through our 'terrible twos.' Infantile. Impulse disorders.

Wars. Manmade famines. Racism, Homophobia, Misogyny."

"Do I have your word?"

Secretariat nodded. "You can trust me."

The specter vanished. Secretariat returned to his birds after saving the planet. Having accomplished this deed, would his inner cultural nationalist stop nagging him? He had given Earthlings some time and this wasn't no movie. Or was Secretariat taking the idea of the

Omniscient author too far?

Chapter 57

A few moments later, Pope Miltiades II and Virginia appeared on a Vatican balcony. A crowd of thousands had gathered. The older people booed and threw things. The young people cheered. They were all wearing their hair in the fashion of the pope's, to the consternation of their elders. They were also wearing T-shirts bearing the image of Miltiades II. But when the pope vanished, leaving only a clump of clothes, everybody fell to their knees and began crossing themselves. The elders as well. He'd been called home to Dido as a result of Secretariat making suggestions to the planet's emissary. That the Didonians didn't need to intervene in the affairs of Earthlings. That the Earthlings had to figure out things for themselves. But the crowds attributed Miltiades' vanishing to an Ascension.

Virginia was depressed for months. Nance felt differently. Maybe she would welcome him with open legs, upon her return to the United States. Maybe he'd have access to that good pussy from time to time. The sweetest pussy on earth.

Virginia didn't require a Deep Sea Driver one only had to slowly slide the tip of his penis into her wetness.

Kinda move it around probing tenderly for her to come. Slowly. She'd make a sound as beautiful as Maria Callas hitting a high note in "Casta Diva." As an old Buffalo Soldier said of Nicole Simpson, "She must have gold and diamonds up there." But Virginia quickly got over her grief when she was offered a multi-million-dollar book contract. Vixen, now an editor at a Manhattan publishing house, was chosen as her editor. John, the former White House butler, was also on her list. All of the weird happenings going in the Jones/Hatch White House had been witnessed by John during his years working as the White House butler. So now he was writing a memoir about the Jones /Hatch Era, as it was being called. He'd received a million-dollar advance for his book entitled *You Can't Make This Shit Up.* A best seller.

Chapter 58

The party had gone on for two weeks. Billed as the last party on Earth, the billionaires and two trillionaires who made fortunes befouling the planet and hogging all of its resources were about to embark to the planet Dido. On this eco planet, resources were plentiful, oceans were on the surface, and the temperature was like Palm Beach year-round. The day to depart Earth arrived. The older men had chosen blonde women on the younger side for their mates. Some as young as ten. They could create on Dido the super race denied to them on Earth. They didn't think that a half-dead Termite Control had the chops to pull off a techno fascist dictatorship. Everyone was strapped in. It would take 300 years to reach Dido, but the spaceship was equipped with gardens and a supply of animals, so an unlimited food and water supply was no problem.

Under an anonymous name, Boy Bishop had taken a room on the highest floor from where he could see the snow-covered Swiss Alps. He could also see the launching pad of the spaceship that would take the billionaires, trillionaires, and others who'd made billions from fossil fuel emissions to the planet Dido.

For them, Earth was a dying planet—useless. He was a data freak. He had memorized the Congressional Report.

> Documents demonstrate for the first time that fossil fuel companies internally do not dispute that they have understood since at least the 1960s that burning fossil fuels causes climate change and then worked for decades to undermine public understanding of this fact and to deny the underlying science. (Denial, Disnformation, and Doublespeak: Big Oil's Evolving Efforts to Avoid Accountability for Climate Change)

Boy Bishop had a briefcase full of clippings. For him these men were beyond Satanic.

"Plastics are everywhere, from the deepest parts of our oceans, the highest peaks on earth, and even in our bodies, causing irreversible damage—in ways known and unknown—to our environment and potentially our health," the Attorney General of California said in a press release announcing a lawsuit.

The lawsuit claimed ExxonMobil deliberately shifted the responsibility for plastic waste to consumers by promoting the idea that plastic recycling was their duty. At the same time, the company knew recycling was not a viable solution.

Boy Bishop looked at his watch. He rose from the computer and went to the window. Through his binoculars, he watched as the spaceship was launched. He returned to the computer and began to type. He'd hacked into the computer onboard the ship, which is why it exploded shortly after take-off.

Calmly, Boy Bishop ordered lunch: a plate of broccoli, a bottle of sparkling water, a Greek salad, and a lamb burger. He was to fly out the following day. Where would he show up next? Who knows? Maybe Iceland? On second thought he remembered having read a news report: *Nov 12 (Reuters) – Iceland has designated the potential collapse of a major Atlantic Ocean current system a national security concern and an existential threat, enabling its government to strategize for worst-case scenarios, the country's climate minister told Reuters.* But then, that would have interrupted his mission: killing the fossil fuels billionaires before they escaped to an eco-planet and carried their evil into space.

Chapter 59

Commissioner Brown was about to leave his apartment to have his daily breakfast with the mayor when a bulletin came across the screen.

Mayor Loathsome Larry had suffered a massive stroke. Commish Brown ordered his driver to take him to the hospital. He rushed to the room where the mayor was receiving intensive care. The policeman who was guarding the room was seated outside asleep. The Commish entered the room. The mayor was asleep too. Commissioner Brown detached all of the equipment that was being used to keep the mayor alive. Then quietly left the room. When he entered the elevator, the Code Blue alarm went off, and as the elevator closed, he could see doctors and nurses rushing toward the mayor's room. Brown entered the backseat of his town car. He asked the driver to take him to a flower shop. There, he bought a bunch of white orchids. Next stop, the cemetery. He laid some flowers in front of his cousin's son's grave. He'd been shot when he was out jogging, while spending the summer in New York between semesters. He had been enrolled in Johnson C. Smith University. His killer was Loathsome Larry, now deceased. As he exited from the gates, Brown's phone rang. It was Boy Bishop. "I told you not to call me at this number. I'm headed toward the car. Call me on the other phone."

Chapter 60

Nance, having found Clift's entourage, was about to check out of the Waldorf Astoria at 1100 Pennsylvania Avenue when he heard a commotion coming from the street below his hotel window. He opened a window and looked down. There was a motorcade passing and people were lined up on both sides of the street, cheering.

First came Cab Calloway wearing white tails, and a wide hat. He was doing his hepcat walk in circles and tossing his straight hair as he danced about a limo carrying Lil Teflon, Michael Protzman's successor. Then came a bubble topped limousine carrying JFK, RFK and MLK, the "Saints" of a million Black homes. The plastic surgeons had done a great job in covering their wounds, which were imperceptible. They waved back to the crowds lined up on each side of Pennsylvania Avenue.

Next came a limousine. Coretta Scott King was sitting in the front. Jacqueline Kennedy and Marilyn Monroe were sitting in the back. They were in conversation. Their feud seemed to be over because they were smiling. After all, both were fans of Ella Fitzgerald. In succeeding cars in the procession were Marvin Gaye,

Tammy Wynette, Princess Di and Dodi Al-Fayed. Miles Davis shared a limousine with Ava Gardner.

Children cheered as a float bearing Kukla, Fran and Ollie, and Clarabell the Clown passed. Mary Jo Kopechne and Dorothy Dandridge, two American martyrs, shared another float. The two saw Nance staring down at them. They looked up, waved, and smiled.

Louis Armstrong, playing King Zulu, passed by on a Mardi Gras float. Then came the The Wild Tchoupitoulas led by Professor Long Hair singing

> Me got fire, me can't put it out
> Heap firewater gonna make me shout
> I'm going down and get my squaw
> I'm gonna buy me a great big car
> I'm gonna do everything I could
> Me, Big Chief, I'm feeling good

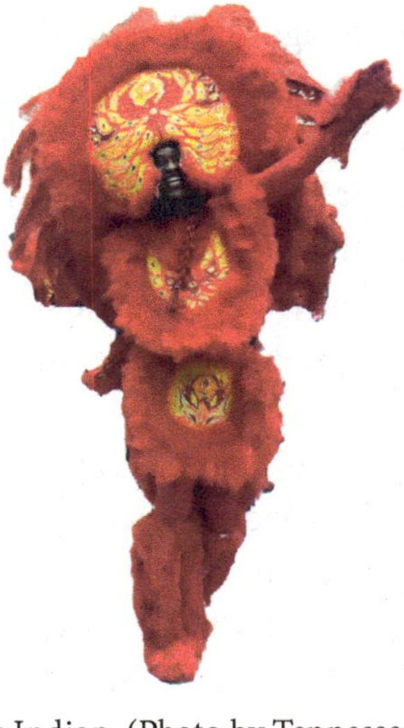

Mardi Gras Indian. (Photo by Tennessee Reed.)

Fred Astaire and Bill "Bojangles" Robinson challenged each other to a hoofing contest. When Bojangles tapped upside a streetlamp and tapped his way down, Astaire who had sung a tribute to Robinson fell to his belly in a salute to his master. Next came twelve bikini clad hunks running while carrying Ayn Rand, the Queen of Selfishness, and now the Queen of Hell.

She was seated on the *sedia gestatoria*, which is Italian for "chair for carrying." The *sedia gestatoria* is a silk-covered armchair that is placed on a suppedaneum. Two large fans made of white ostrich feathers were carried on either side of the throne. Rand was a leading candidate to replace Satan. The first woman. A ceiling breaker.

At the end of Pennsylvania Avenue, the parade lifted off from the ground like Santa and his reindeer when beginning their trip of distributing presents throughout the world. The crowd cheered and applauded until the parade disappeared into space.

Nance remembered his college philosophy classes where they spent hours reading writers who posed the possibility of a variety of realities. But when the students returned to their daily routines, they accepted a consensus about what was real. But just as the onlookers began to disperse, there came a quake in the sky. The day became an arctic night because black energy does not shine. The sun disappeared. There was panic as husbands held their wives. Mothers embraced their children. From the sky, they heard a trumpet that reached a note never before heard on Earth. But it wasn't a trumpet, it was the hotel wake up alarm. Nance had a bad headache.

He remembered that he and Charles had returned to the hotel. They had headed for the hotel bar to celebrate their freeing of Dean Clift's people. They knocked back shot after shot of Jack Daniel's. Nance didn't remember how he got back to his room.

His uncle had said that one of the side effects of the pill was bizarre dreams. The phone rang. It was JQ on the phone. JQ told Nance to come to the office at once. There was a prospective client who was offering them a huge opportunity.

Chapter 61

Barbara and Alice were married. The former NIK cultists had spent only a few months in prison. Andrew and James got them lawyers who sprang them. They were celebrating in Barbara's campaign headquarters. She had just won a New York state senate office, and they had bought a condo in Albany. Outside, it was 23 degrees. Those passing the headquarters were wearing their winter clothes. The sidewalks, covered with crushed ice, were slippery.

Barbara addressed her followers. She was in a good mood. The day before her physician informed her that a tumor they'd found in her gut was benign. She addressed her campaign standing on a table. On the walls were photos of heroes. Shirley Chisholm, Adam Clayton Powell Jr., David Dinkins, Charles Rangel. Louise Thompson Patterson, Hazel Scott, Ruby Dee, and Vinnie Burrows. "With very little money and none from wealthy donors, we've managed to pull off an upset." There was applause and cheers from the campaign workers. "Nobody gave us a chance, but when you take your case to the people directly, as all of you have by standing at subway entrances, passing out pamphlets, going from door to door, all of the lies from the corporate media could not destroy our drive toward victory." Applause. Much hugging. Both Barbara and Alice had lost weight. When they were released, they'd been in the midst of a hunger strike. "We won't abandon our quest to save the oceans, upon which the continuation of human life depends, but what really made Alice and me enter politics was our experience of witnessing the treatment of Black and Brown girls in prison. Why do we continue to hold Black and Brown girls in adult prisons which only adds to their mental health situations? I will end this outrage." There was an enthusiastic response. "One report has it that 'Black girls are three-and-a-half times more likely than white girls to be incarcerated. We will end this injustice." More applause. "Barbaric methods of punishment such as solitary confinement are still being employed. Prisons are being built far away from urban areas and recently, prisons are being relocated to smaller white towns to boost their economies. These women, many of them mothers, lose contact with their children. Alice and I spent a few months in prison during which we witnessed the cruel treatment of women by guards who beat, tortured and even impregnated them but suffered no consequences. We were thrown in solitary confinement for protesting and they shut down our prison newsletter." There was applause. "They objected to our hairstyles, violating the Crown Act which prohibits discrimination based on a person's hair texture or hairstyle if that style or texture is commonly associated with a particular race or national origin." Applause.

"Black and Brown women die because the authorities ignore their symptoms and even ridicule them." More applause. "The food is awful, sometimes filled with maggots, and the prisoners are deprived of sanitary supplies." Applause. "We will close the Women's House of Detention in Greenwich Village, and we will close Rikers Island." Cheers. "Blacks and Browns fare a little better outside of prison. A little better. The absentee landlords rent apartments that violate housing codes, but these landlords ignore citations because they contribute to the campaigns of corrupt politicians." Applause again.

"Now I want to introduce the love of my life. Alice." They embraced. "We left the cult but we still revere the saint. St. Nicholas, the rescuer of exploited women." Alice stepped forward to applause. We are now Democratic Socialists. Seeing that the term Socialist was coined in the United States, what could be more American. What could be more patriotic."

"Yes, Barbara has spoken eloquently about our goals. The conditions of Black and Brown women in prison are horrible, but prison is not the Waldorf Astoria for men." There was laughter.

"Tens of thousands are raped by other inmates and murders are rampant, often encouraged by fiendish guards. In these prisons there is poor sanitation, plumbing issues, vermin infestations, feces-covered walls. Some prisons are controlled by Organized Crime and Nazis. Solitary confinement is used capriciously. Impoverished inmates are there because they are unable to pay bail and have to wait months, sometimes years for their case to come to trial. We will end these problems. And now on to Albany."

Barbara was helped as she climbed down from the table. Champagne was passed all around. They were

Termite and his secret police director, Percy Antman.

leaving their campaign headquarters when a man approached them. It was Oswald Zumwalt. "I'd like to join you in Albany." He handed them his resume. "We'll look it over," Alice said.

Chapter 62

Rev. Mooney and his cohorts had gotten their collaborators in the press to falsify John's reasons for leaving Mooney's mega ministry. Mooney said that he tried to steer John into a positive direction by teaching him about the Lord and he regretted that he had failed. He predicted that John would return to a life of crime.

Llike many Americans, John was disheartened by the state of the country. He thought that the country was at its nadir when the ruling class was a nest of powerful pedophiles, but now, a Necrophiliac, a member of "The Walking Dead" had become the country's leader. American Christianity had become a front for con artists and grifters. First, he had to leave New York,which was slowly burning up as each summer became hotter and hotter.

He rented a room in a California monastery deep in a forest. He needed quiet. To meditate on his next step. He'd finished a spare breakfast, then took a walk among the coastal redwoods and giant sequoias. He listened to the sounds of woodpeckers, owls, and hawks. He inhaled the smells of redwood trees. This forest was threatened with razing by Termite's Secretary of the Interior to use the trees for lumber. This would also threaten deer, bears, squirrels, raccoons, foxes, wolves, bats, lizards, frogs, salamanders, numerous insects, and many species of monkeys.

He came upon a waterfall that was pouring into a river that contained salmon, trout, and Pacific lamprey. The trees, the birds, the animals, the fish, and John had a common ancestor. It wasn't the hallucinogen he took before leaving the monastery that offered him an insight, but it helped. Whatever happened to these living beings would happen to him, but not many members of the human species accepted this idea. Some, like the Raptures, were awaiting the return of Jesus. They believed that Earth has always been, as Sir Walter said of the United States, "brought by the Devil under his fearful servitude," and that only a Judgment Day that would "separate the wheat from the chaff," would straighten things out.

But why hadn't Jesus returned? Because his church was in bad shape? The Russian Orthodox Church was supporting genocide. The Catholic Church was continuing the cover-up of one of the largest sex scandals in human history. Protestant Megachurches had put many mom-and-pop churches, the favorite homes of the spirits, out of business. These Megachurches were regularly hit by scandals, sexual and monetary. Regentrification has sent the Black church, the last holdout for Christianity in America, to the suburbs, where it has lost its urban bite.

California Buddhists had advertised Buddhism as a cool, peaceful religion. Perhaps the Buddhists in

Myanmar hadn't heard of this as they and the Myanmar army killed over 20,000 Muslims. Slavery was still practiced in some Muslim countries. Some adherents to Judaism, the religion of mercy, proved that they could be merciless. Some powerful right-wingers in Israel's cabinet were calling their enemies "animals." The Nazis described Jews the same way. What must he do? What should his mission be? The way he'd left Sunshine Mooney's ministry had caused a scandal. Termite's followers, who had accepted the name their enemies had created for them, "D'Roaches," were tailing him and other enemies of Termite's regime.

If elected, this would be Termite's private military police, who had a larger budget than the navy. They would pour into cities, break down doors, and deport five-year-olds who were on their way to school.

They would challenge the credentials of American citizens. And though Termite had pledged to deport aliens, the military police used the drive authorized by Termite to do some brutal business with Blacks. As someone who humiliated Rev. Mooney, Termite's ally, John's life was in jeopardy. What had gotten him in trouble? Was it his final sermon, delivered at Rev. Mooney's megachurch? It was inspired by Miltiades II's example. When John returned to the monastery, he found the monks huddled around a TV set. He thought that TV sets were forbidden. They were watching Termite's inaugural in silence.

CHAPTER 63

ELECTION DAY

Former Vice President Scab sometimes spelled Scabb left the race, and Ice Cream's father was brought on as Termite's vice-presidential candidate. Termite won the South and the Midwest. Since Termite's policies would hurt these voters the most, maybe you can call them gluttons for punishment? Only a few people from Long Island and Staten Island turned out to see the new president carried on a stretcher and up the stairs to board Air Force One. He was followed by Gut Bomb, Meso, and Gum Shield, the name given to the former cage fighter who, during one bout, had some of his teeth knocked out.

On the way to Washington from New York, the cage fighters had partied so on Air Force I that it took a cleaning crew days to clean up the mess they'd made of the plane. There was an eerie silence at Reagan as they brought the bed on which the comatose president lay down the stairs.

He was greeted by an entourage of distinguished Washington dignitaries and saluted as Termite was carried toward an ambulance that would take him to

Walter Reed's "Ward 71, a multi-room presidential suite where he would be sworn in as president. Only when he emerged from his coma would be moved to the White House.

Chapter 64

The day of Termite's inauguration, there were many flags in the hospital VIP suite where Termite lay in a coma. Only a few members of the press were allowed to enter. Those who met the approval of Gut and Meso, Termite's aides. They had replaced the Secret Service with some retired Octagon fighters, including one who'd beaten his girlfriend so badly she had to undergo plastic surgery. He was out on bail, and Gut and Meso had promised to pardon him. Another had raped a three-year-old child. He was selected as Secretary of Defense.

Outside, there were some protests about a comatose man being sworn in as president, but Phillip Slutt reminded the dissenters that the Constitution didn't require that a president be conscious. Besides, the lawyers who raised this issue were visited by the D'Roaches, Termite's paramilitary auxiliary.

Soon, Termite would have the armed forces at his disposal. And Termite's legitimacy was additionally established thanks to revelations from a man recently recovered from a coma, who said that though he was unconscious in the immediate aftermath of an automobile crash, he remembered being able to hear people around him in the hospital, further justifying the lawyers' argument that Termite Control was aware of his surroundings. A Chinese scientist had come up with a solution. A chip was inserted into Termite's brain. Now he could project his ideas onto a computer, which then appeared on a large screen outside, where thousands of Termite followers were assembled in front of Walter Reed, waving their $1,000 spray cans. A newer model was equipped with lights. It sold for $1500. For $2000, you could not only have a can that lit up but one that played the leader's voice, "I am your exterminator."

At the inaugural ceremony, broadcast to the thousands of Termite's followers who stood in the snow outside of the hospital, Gut Bomb placed Termite's hand on the Bible and Herman Whorst, the Black supreme court justice swore him in. Using the computer through which the comatose president communicated came his answer. That he would uphold the constitution. Those gathered in the suite applauded, including Ice Cream's father, Bruce, who'd been elected as Vice President, and Phillip Slutt, who wrote Ice Cream's father's speech. The Vice President was the first to speak. His speech contained the usual law-and-order rhetoric. Then came Termite's speech. On the screen, they saw the shortest inaugural address in history. The message from Termite in red, white and blue letters: "I am your exterminator." The cheers from outside lasted ten minutes. The thousands of celebrants began waving their Termite Spray cans.

They began singing the white nationalist national anthem, "We'll Have Our Home Again," a song written by Pine Tree Riots. Instead of an inaugural ball,

Termite's followers presided over a burning of books written in English in a Staten Island park. Staten Island was chosen because many of its residents applauded the chokehold that caused the death of Eric Garner on July 17, 2014. His killer, Daniel Pantaleo, is Staten Island's idea of a hero. His defense fund raised $170,000. You could say that the people of Staten Island shared Termite's values.

The next day, the head of the Termite Supreme Court, Black Justice Herman Whorst, said the court would decide whether the Emancipation Proclamation was legal. Termite had accepted a billion dollars from fossil-fuel billionaires and vowed to end alternative-energy proposals, which caught the eye of Boy Bishop, who read the news in *The Guardian*.

Cage fighters from Meso's failed gym filled out the new Supreme Court. Kingsley Scab and members of the New England opposition had been rounded up during the night by men wearing masks and had disappeared.

After renouncing her husband and the Sons of New England as terrorists, former vice president Scab's wife became Secretary of Education. The head of the secret government was also a cage fighter, nicknamed Percy Antman, a tribute to his superior. ability to tackle opponents way above his weight class. He was a strawweight known to knock out heavyweights.

The ceremony became too much for Termite. He communicated his exhaustion through social media, and people were removed from "Ward 17."

A D'Roach at work.

Chapter 65

John the Conqueror thought about his exit from the Mooney's Mega Church while awaiting the arrival of a prisoner who had requested he be brought in to pray with him. Forty-eight hours before, John had given up the riches, beautiful church women coming on to him, and a lavishly furnished home. The Black Pope's Ascension decided for John which train he would catch. Sister Rosetta Tharpe's "Clean Train," not Mel Flores and Cliff Carlisle's "Devil's Train."

> The Devil's train is long and black
> And it's beautiful to see
> It offers you temptation
> It brings you misery.

John was going to continue the Black Pope's work. Give up his kingly living and begin a new church as Miltiades II had done, but apparently, Miltiades was so precious that Jesus had called him home. On his way to preach his sermon, John got the idea for a sermon that would cause Rev. Sunshine Mooney to oust him from his ministry. He, like others, had read about Boy Bishop's escape. His chauffeur had given him the newspaper, which he read on the way. Soon, he was on stage leading a song. Halfway through, he stopped. Dismissed the guitarist who had a mean bass line, the choir, and the dancers. The audience was shocked.

John the Conqueror, standing before a congregation of thousands, had asked for silence. Rev. Mooney and his wife, who sat behind him at every meeting and raked in money to support an extravagant lifestyle, looked at each other quizzically. The audience stopped their amens. Their waving of hands. The Pentecostal dancing.

John began: "How much of a threat was Satan in the scriptures? People gain consciousness because of the serpent in the Garden of Eden. Distinguish between good and evil. Become aware of their bodies. He corrupts Judas, but without the betrayal of Jesus by Judas, there would be no Christianity. Is Satan the co-founder of Christianity? Satan makes life difficult for Job, but God permits him to do so. David yields to Satan's desire to take a census of the citizens of Israel. The census-taking enhances David's reputation. In the Old Testament, God despises vanity unless it's His own. He punishes David with a plague. It is over the top and disproportionate, as usual. Satan criticizes Joshua's dirty clothes, which is a harmless act. He fails to tempt Jesus after promising him the Kingdoms of the World if Jesus would worship him. Satan challenges Jesus's reputation for creating miracles and dares him to jump from a cliff to see whether the angels will save him. Is Satan the founder of logic? Repeatedly, Satan loses in the Bible and falls from Heaven. Though, as some popes contend, he walks among humans, he nowhere threatens to make the planet uninhabitable. The heads of fossil fuel industries are responsible for that. Are they beyond Satanic?"

The congregation began to murmur.

John responded: "Nowhere does Satan threaten conditions that make the planet prone to cyclones, hurricanes more powerful than those in the past. Tornadoes, usually confined to the Midwest and South, are now threatening the downtowns of our Northern cities. Snow in the South. Satan didn't do that. Microplastics are invading the arteries of humans and animals. Satan didn't do that. No ladies and gentlemen, those who are making billions of dollars polluting our planet are the true devils, Satanic, the wicked members of a Christian church that has bottomed out, represented by the man sitting behind me. Rev. Sunshine Mooney." A collective gasp arose from the audience, followed by much chatter.

John persisted, "The real devils are the leaders of the American Christian church." The talk in the audience grew louder. Mooney staggered to his feet. shook his fist at John, named after Blind Willie Johnson's John the Revelator, as one account goes. After several tries to rise, his fat ass fell back.

John continued. "He endorsed a Necrophiliac for president." He turned to Mooney who was glaring at John. "So Boy Bishop might have the right solution." Mooney, his arms folded, nodded at his security guards standing in the wings.

Undeterred, John continued: "You might see Boy Bishop as a villain, but I see him as the angel Michael slaying the dragon of greed. So, Rev. Mooney, I'm no longer going to be your showman while all you do is count the collection money and party. As for you, Mrs. Mooney, eating cake all day while drinking whiskey is not a proper diet." Mrs. Mooney's jaw dropped. Her fixed smile turned into a frown.

Mooney's security guards rushed toward John. He put up his hands. "Whoooaaa, fellas. No need for violence; I'm leaving."

With that, John calmly left the pulpit and walked down the aisle toward the exit of the church. As he slowly walked, he began to sing one of Rev. James Cleveland's songs: "We are Soldiers in the Ar-a-my, we've got to fight although we have to cry."

The Church became silent. The organist, in tears, began to play along. Rev. Mooney, helped to his feet by an aide, lumbered over to the organist, shook him and tried to wrest him from the instrument, but the organist continued playing. Rev. Mooney punched him, yet he continued. John kept singing.

"We've got to hold up the blood-stained banner; we've got to hold it up until we die."

Then some of the church members joined him in song. Stood up and began following him down the aisle. More joined.

Rev. Mooney urged his security to stop the procession, which was growing. More church members joined and were singing:

My mother was a soldier
She had her hands on the Gospel plow
But one day, she got old
She couldn't fight anymore
She said, 'I'll stand here and fight on anyhow.'

The organist kept playing Rev. Cleveland's song, accompanying more church members who were following John out of the church. Mooney called on those bodyguards who hadn't joined to stop the procession, but even they began to join. Mooney ran to the church entrance and tried to stop them from leaving. They pushed him aside, and at one point, he fell down the steps of the church and landed in the streets. He was laughed at by passersby. He sat there bawling. His wife and his remaining aides found him there. "Get Termite on the phone."

Chapter 66

The opening of the JQ and Nance, Inc. office was a success. A few couples were dancing to the pianist's music as the rest of the band packed up. After the couples left, JQ and Nance were alone.

"So why did you arrive so late?" JQ asked. "The guests kept asking for you." She was wearing a black dress that accentuated her features. She was really wearing that dress.

"I felt a little ill. But I feel fine now," Nance answered. JQ greeted that answer with skepticism but replied, "A record producer wants us to track down a musician." Nance found out what JQ meant by "opportunity." They met with the producer the next day.

He was in his sixties. JQ and Nance listened as he told his story. Someone had sent him a tape, and after it was played on several Blues stations, it reached number one on the Blues charts. The return address on the box was listed at a post office in the town of Crinkly, Massachusetts. The sender said he'd wanted to remain anonymous. JQ listened to the producer intently. Nance was leaning back in a chair. The producer indicated that he liked to drink and could use a drink right then.

He'd given up cocaine after spending millions at expensive rehab facilities. At one point he'd spent so much on cocaine that his wife had to obtain power of attorney over his affairs. He was wearing a few thousand dollars' worth of clothes.

"I haven't seen anything like it," the producer said. "The Blues are vanishing or being co-opted. The kids prefer Hip Hop. This tune might save the form." He was the kind of guy who'd rank Mariah Carey over Ray Charles and say that Rock and Roll advanced with the arrival of Mick Jagger and the Beatles. Or that Blind Lemon Jefferson's "Keep My Grave Clean" is important because Bobby Dylan used the song on his first album, or that without Leadbelly there'd be no Eric Clapton, or without Paul Simon, South Africans would never have created a "masterpiece." So here's Leadbelly doing hard time and he thinks, "I really must endure this because without me there'd be no Eric Clapton."

"Strange title, though," JQ said. "My Baby Is a Kinky-haired Indian, Who Loves Nobody but Me." I thought so too. But fans disagree."

"So you say you can't reach the songwriter?"

"That's why I'm hiring you two. I can pay you well. If this guy can write more tunes like this, both of us can make a lot of money." The two conferred for a minute, then told the producer how much money they needed up front. He gave them a big eye-poping check and left.

Chapter 67

The next day, JQ and Nance began their journey to Crinkly, Massachusetts, the location of the post office box. It was about 50 miles from Crinkly when they decided to fill the gas tank. They stopped at a gas station that still had an attendant pumping gas. He was an Indian. While smiling he began a conversation like "Where you folks comin' from?" JQ answered. "New York." The attendant smiled as he replaced the pump. He wiped his hands and approached the driver's side of the car. Nance handed him some cash, a mode of exchange that was disappearing. But there were crude signs at the entrance to the store and beside the gas pumps. "No credit cards." As Nance began to start the engine the attendant asked, "Where you folks off to?"

"Nance replied: "Crinkly, Massachusetts."

"You don't want to go there." JQ asked him why.

"That place is cursed. Nobody goes there." An old man was sitting inside the station's entrance. He had the face of a dried red prune. His arthritic hands were resting on a cane. He had dozed off. "My grandfather knows why. Let me take you to him." They got out of the car and followed the man into the store.

"Grandpa," the attendant began rousing his grandfather, by placing his hands on his shoulders. He awoke slowly to see Nance, and JQ, standing before him.

"These people are headed for Crinkly. You should tell them about the legend," and then turning to JQ and Nance he asked if they'd like some coffee. They answered "Yes," and offered him ten dollars. He refused the money and went to fetch the coffee.

"So why did your grandson tell us to avoid Crinkly, Massachusetts?" JQ asked. Nance could tell that the old man admired JQ's physical qualities. Nance noticed them too, but he wasn't going to say anything about it.

"It's the land of the Kinky-haired Indians," he said slowly and deliberately, eyeing JQ flirtatiously.

"The what?" Nance was looking at a descendant of the Wampanoag tribe who fought the English invaders in King Philip's War. One wonders how the country would look if the invaders had been defeated. Lakes and rivers so clean that you could drink from them without fear of imbibing pesticides or factory wastes?

"So, why should we avoid Crinkly?" The attendant's grandfather stuck out his hand, which had tremors as his grandson handed them coffee in plastic cups. He explained, "He wants you to pay him 100 dollars for the story." Nance gave the old man 100 dollars which he pocketed. The old man began:

"Before white men came to Martha's Vineyard, the Wampanoag were picking blackberries at Duncan's Ridge. When they had finished, they went up on Easterskysser Hill to feast, but one beautiful woman, skilled at medicines, was so busy picking that she stayed behind." He coughed and blew his nose. "As she picked berries, a Black man with thick lips and Kinky hair came towards her. He told her that his chief had an illness that was causing him great pain and weakness. None of his people could cure him. The chief had sent for this medicine woman who with her knowledge of herbs could cure him. They went down a flight of stairs until they came to a land of fruits and flowers. Blacks lived there, and they paid no attention to her as they went about their chores. They had Kinky hair. The man led her to his chief. She asked him to send people to collect the roots she needed. She then created a concoction that cured him. After she cured the chief, she stayed on among the Black people. She made a good business selling her herbs. But there came a time for her to return to her people, and the chief granted her request. The Kinky-haired Indians had a farewell party for her. There was much fiddlin' and dancin'. A Black man proposed to her, but she said she wanted to go home. And so the Black man who brought her to the village took her to the surface and said goodbye. But before he left, he ran his hands through her hair, and it became Kinky like his. She wandered in the forest until she heard a hunting party. Her people. She expected a warm reception after the years of her absence, but instead of their being glad to see her, the chief rejected her because she had Kinky hair.

"The medicine woman wandered for miles until she found a place where she could build a house. She had saved the money she made from selling herbs when she lived among Black people. More Kinky-haired Indians who'd been rejected by their tribes joined her to create

Crinkly. She became known as the mother of the Kinky-haired Indians."

After the storytelling, JQ and Nance decided to drive on to Crinkly, undeterred by the old Indian's warning.

Nance pressed the gas pedal and pulled away from the station. He said to the attendant, "We have a job to do."

"Okay, but don't say we didn't warn you," he replied.

Chapter 68

Nance and JQ drove on a road that ran through the New England forests on their quest to find the Blues songwriter. JQ knew little about the Blues. JQ's favorite music was Jazz. Not the kind that emerged in the 1940s when Jazz musicians were hungry and frequently pawned their instruments. Some played with the great Billy Eckstine band which included Fats Navaro. Gene Ammons. Miles Davis, Dexter Gordon, Dizzy Gilliespie, Charlie Parker and Sarah Vaughn. She preferred Cool Jazz, a reaction to Hot Jazz, from around the time Miles Davis reached his peak in the forties and fifties to his collaboration with Gil Evans, who orchestrated Bebop licks. lush sounds like a musical Sunday. Nothing in-your-face like "Blue 'N' Boogie."

It took Sonny Rollins, Art Blakey, and David Murray to continue the defiant strut of Black masculinity reaching back to predecessors like Ben Webster. Miles was imprisoned by the same chords and extensions that jailed some of the others, no matter how much Bill Evans inverted them. Like Prometheus, John Coltrane strained to escape until his liver was eaten up. But this would not dissuade JQ from her tastes. She said that she got involved with the Death Squad leader because of her love for "Sketches from Spain." She wanted to fuck something Spanish. Nance wouldn't mind fucking her himself, but he'd learned the hard way that you don't fuck where you eat. Still, he'd glance at the movement of her thighs beneath a short dress that fell just above her knees. She knew what was on his mind because when she caught him looking, she'd smile.

When they were thirty miles from Crinkly, there was a sign: "No straight hair after this point." Suddenly, things began to get pretty Nappy. Really Nappy. The trees seemed to be wearing Afros. Nance spotted a goat that was wearing strands of blond cornrows instead of goat hair. This goat was standing next to a tree whose leaves seemed to resemble Jean-Michel Basquiat's hairstyle. The leaves were black instead of green. The fur on some of the animals they saw was Afro-textured. There seemed to be a layer of frizz on the vegetation. They saw their first Kinky-haired Indian walking down the road. They began to see more of the population. Kinky-haired Indians. They stopped in a coffee shop. They sat on stools situated at the counter. An Indian woman with Kinky hair took their orders. Hamburgers, French fries and coffee.

While Nance was attending to the burger, JQ asked the waitress, "Who is she?" pointing to the painting on the wall behind her.

The waitress said it was their founding mother. She further explained: "Because she had Kinky hair, her chief expelled her from the tribe. The legend has it that she became Kinky-haired because a Black man ran his hand through her hair. But her having descendants shows that he did more than that. Pregnant, she'd wandered through the forest until she found a spot where she built her house. Hearing that the founding mother had established a settlement for Kinky-haired Indians, Kinky-haired Indians from throughout America who'd been discriminated against by their racist tribes traveled to the settlement, which had become a mecca for the Kinky-haired, the Wooly-haired and the Nappy-haired, some of whom broke the combs of barbers and were scolded by barbers for having knotted hair. As an act of retaliation, they forbade straight-haired people from entering our town. We Kinky-haired Indians are her descendants."

Nance removed his iPhone and played the tune on YouTube, "My Baby Is a Kinky-haired Indian, Who Loves Nobody but Me." He asked the waitress, "Are you familiar with this tune?"

She listened to the tune, then responded, "Jake Collins wrote that. He comes in here all the time. Here he is now."

A tall, bearded man had entered the restaurant. Even though he had straight hair and was white-skinned, he was greeted affectionately by the Kinky haired diners. JQ and Nance stood up. The two were shocked. Because standing before them was the former president of the United States, Dean Clift. Nance recognized him immediately. "Dean Clift?" he muttered. Clift put his finger to his lips, a recognition that they had identified him correctly. Alive, Dean Clift was a threat to Termite's existence. He would order his men to hunt him down

Goat with cornrows.

and eliminate the former president. Clift was sending them a signal for them to be silent. Clift whispered, "Let me take you to the house. My pickup truck is outside. My sister makes a great blueberry pie. I'll explain everything."

They thought that nobody heard them mention his name, but a Termite supporter, a Kinky-haired Indian who had been appointed by Termite's men to spy on the Kinky -haired Indians, heard Collins addressed as Clift. His job was to report to Gut Bomb in case Kinky-Haired Indians planned to declare war on people with straight hair. For his treachery, Termite would select him to head the Bureau of Indian Affairs. He was seated at a nearby table. He phoned the White House. But couldn't contact FBI head, Percy Antman. He was told that Antman was on a skiing trip. Gut Bomb. Meso, or Cyclo Spora were also unvailable. They were in a suite in Walter Reed Hospital where Luke Lockett, a.k.a. Termite Control, lay comatose. His condition had deteriorated so fatigued was he after the Inaugural ceremony.

The three were watching wrecking balls tear down what remained of the White House while eating McDonald's. In its place, the world's largest Octagon cage would be built. Immigrants would earn their citizenship by engaging in fights with other immigrants. The winner could avoid all of the paperwork involved in becoming a citizen.

Construction had also begun on the Golden Statue of the God Odin.

Outside the restaurant, Clift's pickup truck, with Nance and JQ inside, pulled away. It had begun to snow. Heavily.

Chapter 69

Phillip Slutt was taking some papers to Luke Lockett, a.k.a. Termite Control who was still in a coma. His job was to copyedit the social media that Luke a.k.a. Termite Control, was steadily streaming. Anti-immigrant, racist, misogynist and Zenophobic trash. Slutt dozed off. When he awoke Termite was standing before him. He had disentangled the life support cables. He looked strong healthy. Was he dreaming? Alyab Owo would have to find another nose to occupy.

Termite placed his hands on Slutt's shoulders. Alyab had done some damage because Termite was slurring his words.

"Phillip. You've been one of the most loyal of my aides. At my bedside 24/7. Even though I was in a coma, I was aware of what was going on. I have in mind a higher role for you in my administration." Phillip was so grateful that he dropped to his knees and began licking Termite's hospital slippers. Termite lifted Phillip from where he was groveling. "Phillip, you don't have to lick my slippers."

"But Sir, how else would I show my gratitude?"

"Tell me where the morgue is in this hospital." "In the basement, Sir." Termite embraced Phillip. Phillip could smell the stinking cologne with which Termite doused himself, as he prepared for his date with the dead. Some of the greasy shit with which Termite groomed his hair stuck to Phillip's face. Termite donned a hospital robe and left the Suite.

Phillip was ecstatic. A higher role in the administration. What could that be? But first, he had to tell the world. After all, he was the White House communications director. He made some phone calls. Soon, the news was flashed across the world. Termite Control had come out of his coma.

Phillip was pleased with himself. He threw his chest out. Went to buy a hot dog from one of the street vendors who did a luncheon business near the hospital. He began to sing.

"There's a bright, golden haze on the meadow."

To be continued or have you had enough?

* Of Pope Leo's ancestry, *The New York Times* May 14, 2025, notes: "Joseph and Louise Martinez are both recorded as New Orleans residents on the 1900 census. They had two daughters at the time, Irma and Margaret, and an aunt appeared to be living at their address. All are listed as 'B' for Black."

NOTABLE TITLES FROM BARAKA BOOKS

THE TERRIBLE FOURS
By Ishmael Reed

A JEW IN RAMALLAH AND OTHER ESSAYS
By Carla Blank

EYES HAVE SEEN, FROM MISSISSIPPI TO MONTREAL
A memoir by Fred Anderson
Finalist, 2025 Concordia First Book Award
Silver Winner, 2025 Foreword Indies Award

MY THIEVERY OF THE PEOPLE
Stories by Leila Marshy
Winner, 2026 Danuta Gleed Award for Short Fiction
Finalist, 2025 QWF Paragraphe
Hugh Maclennan Award for Fiction

MISSY WHYNAUGHT
By Elizabeth Ball

NORTHERN GIRLS
True Stories by Michelle Willms

THE GUILT TRIPPERS
A novel by Philippe Mineau

SAINTS REST
A novel by Luke Francis Beirne
2025 Editor's Choice: Maritime Edit Magazine

MIX
Paper
FSC® C100212

Printed by Imprimerie Gauvin
Gatineau, Québec